Dear Readers,

Having presented at Findhorn Foundation and as a longstanding member of the Green Party, I dearly hope what follows will interest you and yours.

This is one of my latest books. ANN OF GREEN FABLES has 460 mini sagas mostly in rhyme, 50 words each. Also included interactive ballads on ecological themes and a potential garden/ park presentation named PAN SPEAKS ON EARTH. This is an adaptation of a real-life sighting in the Royal Botanical Gardens Edinburgh. Possibly in tune with your own publications, for years I've been selling my illustrated cross-curricular books, DOVETALES within in its 10 titles include Godly Geography - Less Green Gloom, More Mother Love...?

Having taught all ages in 4 continents and specialising in creativity across the curriculum, I found that storytelling, humour and the use of bespoke verses often reach places that even chemicalised energy drinks can't touch.

As far as the ANN book is concerned, below please read the proposed blurb on its contents.

Christopher Gilmore
Actor, Author, Teacher, Learner

SPRING UNSPRUNG...?

For reluctant schoolgirl **ANN GREEN**, hope hides in human honesty. Disillusioned by dysfunctional parents and insensitive teachers, she's rescued by her wise and caring grandfather. Together, they become enthusiastic champions of ecological salvation in action, and globally.

As if anticipating the Poet Laureate's request for more grassroots' poetry, these 460 mini sagas are mostly in verse, rhyme giving verve to vital world-wide issues in ways that maybe Simon Armitage encourages.

In these illustrated pages, the miracles of creation are gleefully celebrated while not avoiding in the darker sides, man's greed and the sore lack of earthly stewardship. Altogether, here are holistic ways of harmonising the planet earth's shadowed lungs with the lighter singing voices of ecological field workers; those on our behalf who graft away to save healthy air and environment - for all of us.

Ageless optimism is also explored. It shines through interactive ballads in verse such as '**FROGGIE'S FROGHORN**' and '**FROG IN HER THROAT**' showing how Princess Peculiar got transformed. Oh yes. Please also enjoy, '**PAN SPEAKS ON EARTH**'. A garden play featuring this God of the Elemental Kingdom; a dramatisation of a real-life happening in Scotland - maybe the last refuge of the fairies. After reading '**ANN OF GREEN FABLES**' what inspired miracles might you well achieve now...?

(christopher_gilmore@ymail.com) (07837 971 408)

www.ChristopherGilmore.co.uk
www.ATMAEnterprises.org

ANN OF GREEN FABLES

BY

CHRISTOPHER GILMORE

Cravings of Cosmic Proportions

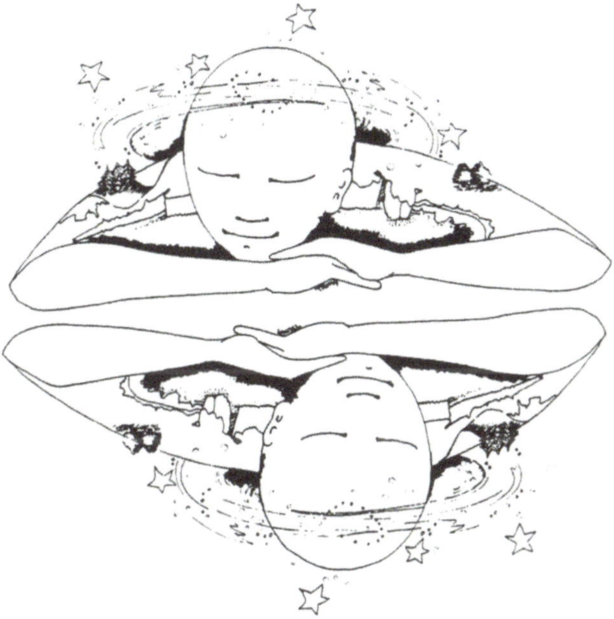

Grosvenor House
Publishing Limited

This book is published by
Grosvenor House Publishing Ltd
Link House
140 The Broadway, Tolworth, Surrey, KT6 7HT.
www.grosvenorhousepublishing.co.uk

A CIP record for this book
is available from the British Library

ISBN 978-1-78623-604-3

ANN GREEN

Fourteen-year-old Ann forgiving Earth
Death with no brief for re-birth
As if Spring is not real or rains on no wheel
Each ship's cabin a sad short-term berth.
Our Ann Green as an early Indigo Lass
In Welfareland leading the mass
Blocks authorities, blooms priorities
Sharing left brain head-talk stale gas?

Original line drawings by

Tony Smith
Mary Macgillivray
Michael Crouch
Clip art

+++

CONTENTS

Dialogues between Ann and her grandad
And in play form
Between Mankind and the Great God Pan
Plus
460 MINI-SAGAS (only 50 words each,
mostly 3 per page.)

TITLES

IN GRATITUDE

May we all thank James Edward Hansen the godfather of climate science.
He first coined the phrase
GLOBAL WARMING – now our shared GLOBAL WARNING.

AUTHOR'S INTRODUCTION

'THERE'S A DIVINITY THAT SHAPES OUR ENDS, ROUGH-HEW THEM HOW WE WILL…'

Such certainties it seems are not in fashion. Yet as the walls of dogma crumble, maybe questions are more consoling than right answers. Especially since one person's right is another person's wrong! Ask, how many question-marks are there in the world's best seller, the Christian's Holy Bible, thanks to felled trees?

Yes, trees I really do thank, together with the busy bees and beavers - environmentalists, researchers, journalists and the like - who, unknown to me, all helped to provide the facts which weave themselves through the planetary tapestry.

These hundreds of verses are all written in the form of the mini saga. The same is true of my series of illustrated inter-curricular books called DOVETALES with titles like 'Godly

Geography - More Mother Love, Less Green Gloom?' Despite many scary facts relating to man and our earth's survivability, I am an incorrigible optimist. Maybe because I see optimism being implicit in the fact of infinity existing and that matter can neither be created or destroyed.

As modern life gets faster and shorter of healthy breath, desperate individuals spend less time, it seems, on simple reflection. The more slippery the slope, the quicker the descent as with increasing ice-avalanches at the Poles. All this less likely to accelerate as good souls raise their eyes above the herds' horizons, helping the necessary rise out of the misery of air pollution, the laziness of litter and the utter lovelessness for 'late planet Earth'...before it's finally too late and our litanies of despair fail to connect any longer with deaf ears. None left on earth.

Is apathy not a sort of inverted anger that has lost its bite?

EARLIER REVIEWS

Since this book like all my work is somewhat controversial, and truth lies in every sincerely held personal view, what follows now are two other reactions to the original – very much shorter – first edition. The following review came from America, sent to me personally from the niche publisher, Helios House. Their rejection read; *Thank you for submitting excerpts from ANN OF GREEN FABLES. I found them interesting commentaries, full of wit and yet also packed with underlying message. I would guess that you enjoy what you do very much. And I would think you'd find a wide international market for your products in this increasingly environmentally aware era.*

I've kept maybe the best review until now. It came from GREEN Print and in part reads: '*...I've been very reluctant to turn this idea down, as it's just the kind of surprise book that might be a roaring success for the right publisher, and I guess it would appeal to the publishing instinct of many publishers...*'

In fact, they don't produce works of 'fiction' although this present version is full of verifiable facts, no matter how uplifting or sad. The many rhymes throughout might suggest the need for more meditation, empathy, romance, fantasy and human harmonies. Yet evergreen idealism needs action as well as reflection.

Now that forty percent of insects have vanished from the bottom of our food-chain, we at the top, that is surely enough to alert more of us. And before more of us become wary of the poisons produced of corporate greed; not least from the international pharmaceutical firms and companies that would entirely colonise, for example, stocks of healthy seeds.

Let's instead lobby for all populations to be well-fed and watered. As for Ann, I like to think she was at the front of truanting schoolchildren's march in order to teach we adults about current shortfalls in practical wisdom as lived by members of, for example Green Spirit and, of course, the GREEN PARTY.

Not that in quiet moments Ann would not be grateful to her grandad's insights. Not least when he suggested to her that the truth behind climate change and reincarnation have much to teach each other by way of a central challenge to out New Age children of all ages.

Now though, I'm happy to thank you for picking up this book whether you stay with it. So over you, kind reader. With Ann and her grandad, I await any feedback, favourable or not.

Again, I quote Shakespeare's Hamlet, Prince of Denmark: -

'…WE DEFY AUGURY: THERE IS A SPECIAL PROVIDENCE IN THE FALL OF A SPARROW. IF IT BE NOW, 'TIS NOT TO COME; IF IT BE NOT TO COME, IT WILL BE NOW; IF IT IS NOW, YET IT WILL COME; THE READINESS IS ALL.'

AUTHOR'S DEDICATIONS

To those folk - maybe like you - who activate their hope in earth's health-giving survival by helping it in practical ways. Yes, to you pioneering midwives of Mother Earth's future, patiently aiming to bring about a better prospect for our descendants, I gratefully dedicate this book, now in its second and much longer, incarnation; and that after thirty years.

I feel love and gratitude when I remember the schoolchildren of several countries who feel, to survive on Earth, they need a cleaner, greener environment, rather than paper qualifications. With the treat of 'species extinction', they are wise enough to know an academic degree is a dead-end if you can't live out a healthy life.

Do we thank the British police for arresting 3,000 people that same week?

Or with me will you thank the self-proclaimed celebrant of Asperger's Syndrome, the sixteen-year-old, Greta Thunberg, a Swedish global hero likely to win the Nobel Peace Prize? She it is who announced, 'We don't have a future anymore.'

And lastly, kindly join me in thanking all the intrepid world journalists, not least those who are being assassinated as 'dangerous' Whistleblowers.

Our survival needs more of them.

YES?

.
.
.

DIE OR SURVIVE?

Thirty million plants and animals are threatened. That means that sixty per cent of world species are threatened with extinction.

History gets longer every day. But all life forms every day can outlive their current limits of earthly consciousness.

Take butterflies. Fossils of these delicate creatures have been found alongside those of dinosaurs, despite Monarchs, our long-range high-flyers now mightily diminished in number. Yet as am ageless symbol of rebirth these delicate insects survived the cataclysmic event that removed from the earth the world's largest mammoths.

Today, some butterflies can fly over the high Himalayas. Whereas the Monarch Butterfly, with a sky-full of others, used to migrate annually in their thousands from Canada to Mexico. Recently, only 10% survive from egg to adult. But all butterflies eat plants that make them toxic to birds. How's that for consciousness responding to the need for species survival? Indeed, without consciousness, how did these symbols of metamorphous, learn which plants digested would save them from predators? Could trial and error be the only reason?

Consider 'snakes and ladders', a game invented by the ancient Hindus who believed in reincarnation. To survive many strategies have been observed, be it that of playing possum or by being devious. Like ground squirrels. They rub the discarded skin of a rattlesnake, its main predator, all over their bodies. This is by way of disguising their own scent in order to keep them safe from death.

How could such squirrels, unless with more consciousness than rattlesnakes, be that sneaky without some inner guiding awareness at work, self-conscious of not?

Take the eastern corral snake. Its deadly venom can kill with only one strike. A distinctive livery of alternate red and black bands extends all along its body. In contrast, the scarlet king snake is harmless. Though defenceless, the coloured rings around its length are so like its poisonous rival that both snakes mostly remain safe from their shared enemies, coati and foxes. Again, how could such a devious disguise exist without consciousness at work?

INSECTS

Even the seemingly lowest of animals, like the beetle species, have developed chemical weapons. This defence system applies to one of the smallest, the soldier beetle. Preserved in amber, it's now known to have been alive and thriving in the time of the dinosaurs. Yet then as now, a gooey sap oozing from its abdomen spreads all over its tiny body for this toxin to prevent a beetle from becoming a meal. How could such a defence system have developed in such a tiny mite without consciousness?

However, there are no reports of the beetles' toxins being deployed to gain any worldly advantage. It is used only when threatened with an attack. Though millions of beetles, unlike humans, are more likely to survive nuclear warfare, despite their consciousness being no way as fully developed as that of the human soldier.

Yet it seems that consciousness exists throughout the entire food chain on earth and, arguably, *beyond* as well as *before* incarnating. Such innate gifts are shared by our animal neighbours. For example, camouflage and shapeshifting as well as defensive chemical weapons already mentioned. All such protective strategies are prevalent throughout the animal kingdom working as instinctive reflexes. Unlike, that is, the consciousness in humans. Amongst us, even those less mature have conscious choices and can be aware that every choice has its consequence.

By then, they may fear their own near-death. That's if they'd not been eaten into extinction by manufacturing mankind.

As for the equation of *survive or die*, scientists are still discovering about the inner connections interlinking all animals, including the hundredth money as with we humans. Responding to the triggers of fight or flight, animals do not seem to fear death. Instead, they seek to preserve is their own species, whatever their personal cost. While the nutritional value of dinosaurs has not been fully recorded yet, even that if hummed cannibals in caves, sewer rats can nourish us, if we're in need of food. For example, 3.5 ounces of rat flesh can provide 21 grams of protein. Contrast that with beetles. They provide up to 36 grams of protein per 3.5 ounces giving us calcium, zinc and iron. That is 15% more than rats.

No matter what physical differences exist, all animals are seemingly rising up the scale of awareness by sharing a group consciousness This helps their species to survive; not just that but incrementally, and to develop a corporate potential. Think the hundredth monkey syndrome. As a breakthrough it illustrated how their genus was advanced by refining a seaside eating technique, distance being no barrier, as also in telepathy. Somehow, mysteriously, new levels of awareness can, as it were, travel a hundred miles over the sea to help the practical survival of their own kind on another island.

Back to rats! In a Scottish caravan park, the founders of the Findhorn Foundation had under their beach caravan a family of rats. The vegetarian wife tuned into the diva of that species and asked for them to leave. Next day they all did so. For years they remained absent. Yet the day the adults left the caravan, rats returned. As pets, rats can become both loyal and intelligent companions. Also, cats, these said to have nine lives.

I had one such pet that over a period of thirty years, returned to me three times. In each new body it had similar marks as if to signal the return of the same Soul. Not only me, but it also I believe consciously shared with me the experience of déjà vu.

Animals can teach us much. Instinctively, as Soul, in not fearing death they seem to know we all survive more than one life. How well this is illustrated by the lives of snakes, frogs and butterflies. These creatures in one lifetime morph through a series of many bodies – symbolising the continuum of all of life's energies whatever its form or lifestyle and temporary physical needs. Indeed, animals have inspired many poets; more so maybe, then minerals and plants. But Rumi, the Persian writer, was inspired by all life-forms on earth.

As for our present species, if we humans see global Armageddon as a gateway to a safe future, it might be worth mentioning that more of mankind has trod on the moon successfully than have sailors managed to circumnavigate their adventurous voyage around Africa's storm-battered Cape Horn. Unlike many fish.
Part one of Rumi's verses reads –
I died as a mineral and became a plant;
I died as a plant and rose as animal;
Why should I fear? When as I less by dying…?

Not so much survive or die but die and survive…?

SEASONS

As the frosts begin to nip, seared leaves soon lose their grip.
As winter snows abound, new bulbs are breaking ground.
When the lambs no longer suck, each drake soon scores a duck.
When the birds and bees have done, their holiday's just begun.
For different seasons many reasons.

STUCK?

'I shouldn't have black hair!'
'Change your tune, Ann. That's at least 500 times you shouted that.
You don't have black hair - so there!'
'Did before...'
'Before what?'
"And will again, you wait.'
Ann poured a tin of treacle all over her head.
Sticky business, not being believed

RABBITS?

Let's agree, rabbits can't read
So who taught bunnies how to breed?
For as far as we can guess
The doe says always "YES!" Always her luck to fall
She can't pass the buck at all.
To us there seems but little doubt,
The rabbit is a litter lout.

TIP OF THE ICEBERG?

From rubbish Ann was always making treehouses, mobiles, jewellery, ornaments. Until Ann was ordered to concentrate on her weaknesses, reading and writing. She did and they got weaker.
Soon Ann ran away, shivered in a rubbish-tip, waiting for burial.
Even though biodegradable, the Council did not offer to recycle Ann.
Cutbacks.

TOUCH WOOD

'When William Caxton published the first lady
author, *The Muggers'*.
It's said protesters wrapped themselves around
trees to save them.
Trees are thanked for oxygen, garnishing parklands,
obliging dogs, making fires, totem-pole, pit-props, leaf
mould, weapons, furniture, Conkers and for climbing. But
sadly, they can't save themselves from us, Ann.'

BREATH

'All-round inner and outer good health
Rate higher Ann than bad wealth
Feeling fine in fresh air I feel rapture
Science now onto carbon capture
Though storage or dispersal problematic.'
'Grandad, Mother Nature's got her own solution
Like me autistic with outer and inner pollution"
'She's no sinner just asthmatic'.

MAN-u-FACT-URED?

Manmade hurricane the size of all France
Fossil fuelled finance fanatics advance
Marching over soil seeking future oil
The Caribbean spoil conquering oceans, as if walking on waves
Pounds' Power their impoverished peon.
Most free energy buffs in premature graves
Darkest rumour-monger joins subscribers
Many getting drugged by conspiracy prescribers.

FREEZE FIGHT FLIGHT?

Leaves on branches above in light
The roots of trees in dark all fight
For sustaining soil as yearly rings coil
Love over ground leaves fears out of sight
As mother ferrets feed dead mice
Mother Nature not all ways nice.
"Ann if deaths don't exist should killing suddenly desist?"

BALANCE

Invisible roots oxygenating leaves
Imitating egg times shaped wheat in sheaves
Upside downside balanced for stability
Lessons for all of us with disability
Agreed by those with ecology on wet sleeves
Before good global health from our planet leaves
Homes flood as rain roams free…Saved by each town tree.

OM-NI-ALL?

Isn't odd that God's everywhere
Deep within seas as well as in the air –
Everywhere?
God is here, God is near
God's clear in all we love
That flows from way above
Each to their due, through me and you,
Through all the beauties of repartee
Talking to a tree.

DREAMS

If birds got vertigo on high. no poisonous snakes would fly
Allowed by Divine Right worlds end up in flight
After multiple eons fly by…!
Worms dream of holes, not mouths of moles and their fat girth;
Dream of a loving end to their low life,
Well-removed from landlocked earth.

CONFLICTS

Normally all's dead in Ann's fridge
Yet hanging on elastic thread spiders not dead
How can it live without a midge?
Condoms guns nicknamed protection
Both permit people's vast deduction
Fewer folks to kill fewer mouths to fill
Ann praises gays for people reduction
Plus celebrate Priests not ravenous beasts.

FAITH

'Love all creatures with care
Ann to how many do you respond?
Badgers' and hedgehogs' roadkill less
Than high-rated bright birds and Rupert Bear!
With litter-pickers on the road,
Allow Angels to lighten your load
Outbrave all bad storms, find help.
Faith needs bold forms,
For blessings we're owed.'

SURVIVING?

'Let voices and visions bring light. Let others get frazzled
with fright
As neighbours complain your family's insane
Ann keeps inner certainties in sight
Forgotten like an old granny on ice
Mother Nature has a large price
Her only way is health's green goodwill.
Health, not cash is generous wealth

DINOSAURS HEAVY DRINKERS?

'Engravers love carved hearts on trees
See graffiti fossils that freeze.
Large footprints on Skye. As time marches by
Imprints and dragons deeply impressed

Dinosaurs drank from our springs
Short-lived as evaporation and Mayfly's wings.
Ann better not to think that's what we still drink
But bless all that life brings.'

FAIRY TALES?

Perched on their favourite tree
Sheffield birds tweeting with glee
Now much stronger their songs last longer
Council saved from idiocy.
Yet still Amazon jungles weep.
As deep well-oiled shareholders sleep.
Money concerns palmed-off the new rich a toff
It's capitalism's greed
While pollution creeps less goblins breed?

BIRD BRAINS?

Good love seen paraded less need for hearts be jaded
With squirrels in parks love's much more than sparks
Best feelings not blockaded
Leave food for the tool-wielding crow
With fruitful hedges all will still grow
Profits won't sustain land where bad chemicals go
Let birds on pure thermals flow

MICE AND MEN

South for sun and North for ice.
Both suit mankind when less than mice
Continental drift? Progress needs a rift.
Temporal things can go in a trice.
In every village a Wi-Fi parochialism if precious as Pi
Or Global Embrace all countries save face.
Proactive action can widen the sky?

DEVELOPMENTS?

Makers of plastic we still cajole.
See plastic goldfish in plastic bowl.
Deep sea fish ingest Dead plastic won't digest.
Let the bells of hell on earth toll.Plastic bags garland dolphin necks.
Developer our home planet wrecks.Violence seems often rewarded
As if sweet Peace Ann can't be afforded.

SOUND SENSE

Rosetta Comet as our dear sun's swan song
Data logged before it invisibly gone
The Celestial Choir fuelled by God's fire
Without Space race telethon!
Nearly 1 in 20 rare species dying
Sad struggling conservationists sighing
Ann feeds homeless sees pesticides a sin
Survival for all life forms is death defying?

GROWTH

Ann says, "Icebergs bomb on desert sands.
Gobi Sahara need fertile lands
Our Good Earth revives if goodness arrives
Healings hedge herbs help together with kelp
Ann finds activities love improves
Serving what's stuck in sour grooves
Let's change our view unstick cosy glue
Lowest mountain knows how Gaia moves.

CAUSE-EFFECT

Fight for ideas with guns and knives.
Violence as power nearly thrives.
Force karma's boomerang assuring mutual bang
Thank God we have so many lives?
Insights not near, afraid they'll get clear,
Ann sometimes you yearn
For what's left to learn.
Your mission won't yet go dark in solar-roofed Ark?

HUNDREDTH MONKEY

Two days since jokey poachers taunted monkeys, stoning
The bravest to death and killing the oldest with their
Landover,
The men in yellow T-shirts.

Driving through a neighbouring jungle, the yellow
poachers were attacked. 100 monkeys jumped their vehicle,
hairy fists smashed their weeping windscreen

CLEANLINESS

'Clean clouds clearing more light shows.
Love your truth Ann the more it glows. 'Migrating
songbirds lack jet-lag. No beer breaks or fag?

'Heart burning for a fertile guest a wicker ashtray Robin's
nest
His first flirty Bird said, "Stop smoking in bed!'

Joked he, "So knit me a fireproof vest!"

GROSS

Fried food or pate to fuel some fatty
All dead feathers as rags
Public litter louts should get copped
Plastic bottles and bags not dropped
Flesh not sustained, then what is gained
If chock full recycling plants get blocked? Money measures?
Plenty plus gives small pleasure.
Wisdom's health not wealth?

WRONGS?

Forest and folks' degradation, sensitives needing sedation
Global green prizes our homeless despises. Housing not on
the Human Rights' Charter like habitats for wildlife.
Reform of wealthy powerful a non-starter.
Social justice attained through stealth?
Weather controller's spells might fill water wells
But beware black magic when too often wet?

CONSUMERISM

'Bloated bats share insects with bats' failed hunters.
Ann make ponds for frogs, burn less logs.' Two Potters
wrote While thanking trees' habitats and nooks Not flesh
and blood.
Ann believes Creation makes all creatures from mud
Life kindly boosts what's lovingly produced
Holy Cows chew all kinds of cud!

HOW FAST IS SLOW DEATH?

Taken from the author's Dovetales Godly Geography

Half a million hedged verges in GB. Sporting wildflowers to
feed the burrowing bee. Many million miles of tar entomb
earthworms to free the car.
Fewer woodlands for killing blood sports. How many
oil-tankers to choke reeking ports?
Hamburgers with B.S.E. before God's milk and honey
Become avoidable tragedy …?

POWERS

As methane gas sours the sky
Earthbound creatures try not to die.
Some birds don't migrate junk food now their plate,
Fat African Storks can't fly.
Wishing is stronger than iron, imagination more than lion.
Invisible powers fuel flowers
Wishing-bone flight empowers
Its flexibility gives rise so each bird flies

CRUEL TO BE KIND?

On worldwide nutrition day Jamie Oliver keeps sugar away.
For materiality don't pray.
Get healthy and strong all sing one health song
As sweet multinationals' hold sway
Like greedy weeds and gales that slay
Mother Nature's whip on naughty mankind
Cruelty assigned as deaf and blind
By some Deity designed.

NO JUDAS KISS?

Red squirrels endangered not grey. Pandas and pastures
less profitable than Bonds? Like life-supporting unpolluted
village ponds Rainbows and dragonflies' kiss,
scorpions and python's hiss.
All life forms linked till icebergs extinct.
Town sparrows or sparrow-hawks are they missed
If no-one and nothing born bad.
Ann be joyful soulful and glad!'

INVISIBLE

Blame childhood like weather
Lessons blessings altogether
Optimism ties no tether
Consider patients never seen
"I check what's on this scree," says blank Doctor Pills
Insides spawn ills unseen
Hence spirituality known as green loves gardening on knees
No town allotments or fruit trees
Near schools hospitals housing bees.

TOOTH AND CLAW

It snaps hard on moles and mice
Barn owl's beak a hold fast vice
Cat's jaws plus sharp tiger's claws
Make Nature's Laws not very nice?
Yet why poor folks are still unfed
And why's the food chain filled up with pain
More than eating a full breakfast in bed?

LESSONS

'Tooth and claw the ways we learn
Too much fire we all burn
Forest folk turned to black coke
All creatures taking turns to choke
Questions like kids come into to play
If answers silent as we pray
While mankind demands his way,
Ann need manmade problems come to stay?'

HORATIO

See every problem as a quest
Challenge treat as a chosen guest
Cure what we cause.

Too much rush needs a pause.

Bring spirit mind and body rest invisible energies all mesh.
Belief in elementals helps to see life afresh and new
Fairies in Findhorn Bay garden drink morning dew?

PHYSICS?

'Positive and negative polarities?
Father Time and Mother Nature sexed by a needle and thread
As your granny did as its movements she read.
It swayed into a circle each time her womb tested.
As in that old wives tale nightly she invested.
Demoting science
Needs wise defiance.

TACTICS

Virtual Reality trades in fakes
Factory made flowers causing mistakes
While bees not deceived
Sweet nose sniffing sneezed
Not nectar but house dust in flakes!
Cuttlefish use disguises
Ferret rabbit hypnotises.
Cockbirds don't know their broody hen has a lover.
For prey some spiders hide undercover.
Beyond praises Nature amazes!

TICKERS

'Tell my fob-watch time doesn't exist,' said Ann's grandad as
if to insist. 'Nature recycles. Anything missing from this list
shout out, girl.
'Why's my horrible straight hair not curly?'
'All's well. Ask sacred geometry with psychometry.
This watch shares my energy
We're both working co-ops...
...until my heart stops...'

HIGH-HEALED

Volcanoes geysers earthquakes continental drift.
In a duel universe many a rift. Aim all anomalies to sift
What's static needs to shift Nature's never still
With no doctor's bill, all is self-repairing.
Like our own bodies if healing due.
Yet climate change is nothing new
Without change nothing grew.

VERSATILITY

Octopuses and crows, these bird
Architects brighter than kids of 3.
Animals solve problems with no degree
Moulding soft moss nest is jenny wren
Showing intelligence beyond our ken.
Lyre birds an orchestra, bats with sonar
Loving Creator Life's donor.

Creatures fear not death in every deed
All living to breed.

HEALING TREES

Tuning into trees' healing quintessence
It's like bugging their secret essence.
Unlike spirited boys mugging horse chestnuts for conkers.
To the profane worshiping trees seen bonkers
But Beverley Nichols cured cancer tree-hugging.
With healing properties, hawthorn alder yew
Piping cosmic energies to you.
Is the Green Man Nature's god, Pan?

PERFUME

Chemical warnings shiver all trees.as boys
Attack conkers innocent woodland's seeded toys
The largest fell scuttling under a leaf
Safe from meat-skewer much relief
Thanks to Nature Spirits helping to build each chestnut
tree
Till foliage with shining blooms growth fulfilled.
'Heaven-sent for free. These humans hear Ann as scent.'

EVOLUTION'S LINKS

Minnow envy angelfish. Flying Ann's Soul's wish.
When a tree, not free. Bored roots dreamed of advancing
As a crane Ann yearned to improve her dancing.

In baby ballet, she'd supernatural gifts, loving fish, birds,
trees. Grandad watching, all these are all joy bringers,
All flourishing under her green fingers.

FAIRIE KINGDOM

Pan manifests when earth awareness on a downward arc.
As FRIENDS OF THE EARTH have often sensed.

Volcanoes can't be fenced

All nature wants to expand: Hills wish to be mountains
And shrubs trees; seeds flowers; showers floods; floods clouds

Man plans beyond tropso/pause/strato/ion/spheres -
Counteracting fears.

PIPER

Assassinate all rats man's rotting waste will mount
Nuke every plant, green or toxic, corpses will mount
True Saviours don't save us from freewill
Soul not dead when Life Force say, 'Be still.'
Rich folk with fiscal shares in fatal fossil fuels thrive
Buzzing with superior glee unlike the beehive.

UPON THIS ROCK

63-year-old Robert Ogilvie Crombie in Rosemarie seaside
town tuned into a sparkling waterfall tumbling down.
On flat stones three gnomes suddenly appeared.
Boy Roc had dropped a penny in its wishing-well.
Bubbles showed his wish they'd tell
Fairyland to reveal their unseen.
Findhorn's magic garden - now green as a bean.

ASTRAL EYES AND EARS

Edinburgh's Royal Botanic Garden
Roc at Zeiokova Canpinifola, the spirit-talking Tree of Life
A horned faun carved on its bark.

Back resting against trunk, Roc felt a
forceful electrified mist.
'Remember me at Edinburgh Festival?' asked Pan's
unearthly voice.

'I sat next to you during ethereal
A MIDSUMMER'S NIGHT DREAM.

EXPLOSIVE?

Mankind sits on bombs like eggs in clutches.
Stockpiles protected by rabbit hutches

130 tonnes plutonium in Cumbria West
Half-life of 20,000 years lasting at best.
Live cancer embodied in babes unborn.
How long before GREENPEACE sees no dawn?
Breast milk and berries radioactive.
Once Paradise was gloriously attractive

EVERLASTING?

Which wildlife will survive accident-prone mankind?
As we still live through nuclear threats deaf and blind
Be it crabs beetles cockroaches and rats as survivors go bats?
Cull 150,000 cows to rescue New Zealand herd
Curbing methane breaths but have you heard
Chernobyl wildlife not folk thrive there undeterred.

PROFITS OF DOOM?

What money-loving polluters are profit haters?
Fair Trade Good Energy invest in renewable generators
Smart solar sites make pioneering futures greener
Less fossil fuels emitting all surroundings get cleaner
Less respiratory deaths figures collapsing
No diesel and petrol fumes now lapsing.
Without oil-spills no cormorants choking
No train-drivers stoking coal.

SUNLIT LIFE

Lion of Light links all rays' golden rules through all dark days
Sun god in many ways,
Lets atomic powers bless flowers
Moon our mirror to reflect upon, for man's feet a marathon
Running from feeling mad.
Let every lass and lad thank it for hiding when night has gone.

PREDATORS

Crystals alive sparkle in black ice.
Unique snowflakes don't appear twice.
Reborn snowstorms' shapeshifting forms
Hide mountain predator.

Despite dangers from climate changes fractured family far its ranges.
Lofty snow leopard lacks indigenous genetic diversity.
Starving killer poachers also climb bald slippery
plant-grazed slopes Nearly 18,000 feet despite shared adversity.

GENERATING GALAXIES

Ever-expanding ever shapeshifting
What eggs would hatch birds' life-long sitting?
Organic particles electrifying particles
Larger atoms singing like infant planets
Eons before circled by articles
Or earth's warden feasted on gannets
Till James Lovelock extensively interlaced
Love's links in life's webs all temporarily placed
Trillions star-like cells each galaxy swells.

UNSTABLE COSMOS

Mother Gaia evolving into balance and order
Rational science with repeats tests reason's border
Supernatural inborn consciousness in all life-forms
Quantum physics now redefining past notions shed
If gemstones heal how does Stonehenge if inwardly dead?
Intermingling vibrations enhancing all inter-species'
relations
Ann rejects objective approach, Grandad her subjective
Coach.

INNOCENT JUICES?

Smoothies' woolly hats for those old alone
No car oil more ecological by phone
Clean firms allot roles like Last Lever Levers
Fresh Air Lights pleasing green fairy devas
Saving non-essential power both night and day
By opening windows instead of air-conditioning
And Legionnaires disease.

Let global good health stay.

GENE POOLS

Not dinosaurs but flying unicorns on the Astral Plane?
Though mammoths, scientists aiming to
reincarnate them again
With dodos developed from turkeys' DNA?

Horse-pox now in labs today
With jellyfish inside a researcher
Hoping like Hitler for a perfect race.
Image a female ape with chemical makeup on its face.

DOOMSDY CLUB

Addressing man's might they reckoned
It was 7 minutes to Cinderella Armageddon's nuclear midnight.
Since Last Trump blowing hot and Cold War
Not a 4-minute warning before
120 seconds of countdown to no left breath
Walls around rich golf courses won't save
Manicured lawns
From the stench of universal death.

LOOPY LESSONS

Tooth and claw how we learn.
Too much fire we all burn.
Forest folk all turned to coke
As every creature takes its turn.
See each problem as a quest
A challenge less a pest.
Cure what we can cause,
Faith found in a pause bringing
Body minds meditations' healthy rest.

RESERVOIS, AU REVOIRS?

Tree of Life, its leaves flapping like flags on a sinking ship?
Elf King warns, 'Upset nature's balance,
Your mankind's murderous parasites destroying spoil
Killing species and our harmonious cooperation.'
Easy to see good deeds, less easy accepting bad ones?
Change before you drown more fairy glens, our green dwellings.

ON EARTH PAN SPEAKS

(Full outdoor play later)

'See my cloven hooves, shaggy legs & goat's horns,'
said Pan to Roc.

The Church called me the devil,
All pagan gods into fiendish imps.

'Play your pipes, please,' requested Roc.
'To see elementals integrate
Your lower and higher selves.
Training takes years longer
Than that of a brain surgeon.

BIRDWATCHING

Bonny colourful buoyant with song
Flying eyes seeing no food as wrong
Danger from predators and rivals' greed
Prey and victims urgently breed.
Their matins and evensong.
Nightingale's lullaby all night long.
Countryside's sounds and odours soothed by grass and
trees,
These all ease mental pains more than gin-and-soda?

CYCLES

Reptiles are solar powered
Without sun which bloom flowered
How similar are sunrise and sunset?
Penguins and storks' songs greet downlight
While well below circles the large-clawed kite
Over trees' unseen rings spiders weaving their net
Soundwaves spiralling their spread
On circling planets too much
The sun's dead

IN THE BELFRY?

Moonlit or in dark as dogs bark
Bats swerve and drive swoop and arc
A range of bleeping squeaking
Blind eyes with mapping ears seeking
Evening Insects to consume before finding room
Upside-down beams their floor
Sharing with their underfed peers as volunteers
Half their food intake for survival's sake.

STEWARDS

Above earth for 52 million years
Before scientists brought fears
Blinding bats blocking their ears
To prove how they move
Their cries louder than pneumatic drills
Bats were tortured to reveal their skills
Boosting deaf & blind researchers' job chances all agree
Animal lovers would have given quicker answers for free.

CAPITAL

After 3.5 billion years
Melting honeypots of worldwide ethnic inhabitants
On this over-island. Mayor bankrupt of cheaper solutions,
homeless Beggars common as crack...infested garages...
Bewildered men under the ticking eye of Big Ben.
Good ideas are cheap as kindness
Spare enough for one. Share enough for all.

SUICIDE PACT

Chewing human hamburgers Victor Vulture had a brainstorm.
'Let's develop weapons that can destroy all history"
'Husband, humans already have.'
'You mean this Chernobyl corpse is for the lav?'
'Precisely, darling,' said partner gravely. 'The world's a wreck.'
Then far too ravenous to commit suicide sooner
She nibbled his decaying neck.

FEEDING THE BIRDIES

No bread feed coots, duck, garrulous geese (immigrant)
Stately swans
See seagulls after the robin bobbing on the spade
Cause flights.
Odd how greedy geese attack hissing geese,
Yet no fights with ducks, moorhens, grebe...anglers.
A tramp jumps in…
Strangles a goose,
Grabs from the bank a bag of Breadcrumbs…
…and runs...!

See 'WATCH THE BIRDIES' by this author!

EVEOLUTION

How much poison-ivy
Fatal before being left
Untouched alright…?
How many apes
Since they substituted flight for fight...?
Stress comes not from pressure but from wrong decisions.
'Did God cook Creation, mixing all ingredients?
Without consulting a recipe book…?
"Einstein's EUREKA happened in a sunbeam, Ann.'
Not a classroom.'

LAPLAND

Is Father Christmas a Billionaire?
Overused stocking beyond repair?
If icebergs were gold who'd drown in rising prices…?
Do market forces reach their own level safely?
As a hole in the pocket or ozone layer…?
When seawaves lap round Primrose Hill
And puffins nest in Big Ben
What price the City's liquid assets…?

GLASNOST

Alaska, grey whales were trapped in acres of ice.
International aid from both sides of the Cold War,
Eskimo-led.
Militia risked hyperthermia.
A long corridor of man-made snow-pierced windows
With hopeful air-holes heading off not into the Hollow
Earth's heaven...but oceans their home!
Friends beware - whale-killers await you there.

ALTERNATIVES

Which the more dangerous, droughts or acid-rain and
floods or lastly, a spark from St. Peter's warning, - 'The FIRE
next time!'
Which is crueller, rats or rockets, religion or rabies;
Cannibalism or capital punishment, animals in zoos and
labs…
Or political dissidents in jail…?"

Bomb deserts
With Icebergs
Or die?

NEWS

'He's horrible! With car-crashes, the more killed grandad,
The louder he cheers. Loves disasters. The pound drops no groans.
He grins. Plane crashes he's happy as Larry. More food, he says.
Last earthquake he was Jumping Geronimo.
What's wrong with him, grandad?'
'Ann dear, caring deeply can hurt too much.'

RAT RACE

'Wanna LOADSAMONEY!'
'Rude to teachers...poor attendance...punctuality… suggestions...?'
'Cooking.' 'Executive chefs worse than Head teachers.'
'Then Uncle Mac's. Plumbers. Apprentice?'
"Start the bottom, arse'ole!' he told me. Sewer-workers earn more than what do teachers, shitface. Upwardly mobile, me, killing fat rats, said Uncle Mac."'
'Ann don't listen to him. Nepotism? Education wasted…'

POWER

'Which live wire is stronger, the negative or positive, Ann?'
'What happens when they're earthed, grandad?'

'People are lightbulbs or lampshades. Beacons show the way
like you Ann, while darker folk try to lessen the light Lose
the way for both types. People can either illuminati or kill.'

'Like electricity.'

DUSTBIN

'Everything old, Ann, gets untidy. Like Britain. Lethal litter,
plastics choking seas, sands, soils, air and water.'

'Earth's a granny glued to her own grotty potty, Grandad.
Even our Playground's filthy - kids!'

'Ann, whatever we Cause we can cure.'

'Kill litterbugs? How many dead coke cans make a tank...?'

LIGHT

'Grandad, offer me some glimmer in all this green gloom
'Light a candle, child. Now blow it out.
Listen. Where' is it still flickering…?'
'In my heart.'
'Indigo! What keeps it alight through all winters' long
nights, Ann?'
'Loving all life.'
'And what snuffs out love, Ann?'
'Fear.'

CABBAGES

'Green voters have ALLOTMENTS!'
'On remaining playing-field, Ann? Tell that science teacher
polychlorinated biphenyls 30 times too high. Teach
pollution prevention, not redundant...'
'My football team too thin, Grandad. Leave stuff....'
'Pupils clearing up? Farmers forced to clean up land
contaminated with chemicals.'
'Who pays if they don't - Prosperity?'
'Posterity.'

STAIRCASE

'Why wait for spaceships? Travel now, that's what advert said, sir. Can we go now, please? Like meditation, going into inner space??'
'PASSWORD?'
'VENUS!'
'Too young, Ann. Not now. Best try later...'
The child with golden speckled eyes sneaks into an interview room.
She waits...and waits…
She's still waiting.

BUILDING BLOCKS

'My escapee Iranian friend was taught good science, Ann. From pure basic principles upwards, step-by-step. As so with maths. Unlike here where teachers feed you old worksheets covering only the tip of the iceberg, not the underlying wonderful marvels of life's creativity…'

'Grandad, let's go there now…!'
'And get ignored?'

BY NUMBERS?

'Grandad, that Doctor's old maths book. Could only answer one question. Then praised himself asking for a week's salary.
Seeing me shrug, he boasted he'd PhD in physics.'
I may be young but know a cheat when I see one'.
'Ann, my university lectures then were never ever Dumbed down.'

CONQUERING KING

'By Divine Right, we can turn the tides of time.'
'Age must wrinkle thy face, Father. Oh, thou art frowning.'
'Ageless ocean, obey my kingly command - tides RETREAT!'

'See Sire, wet feet. Weeping will not help thy
throne's rising damp.'

'This monarch will NEVER age.'

'Nay daddy Canute - only drown…'

STOP PLAY

'Sports' champion, heroes, faces on old cigarette-cards? '
'Tee-shirts, Grandad.'
'Football tribal warfare, today's religion? Competition
attracts ungenerous egotists. Illicit drug-users false good
news. Silicon-fattened breasts?' He disconnected
phone. 'Sorry, Ann.'
'Football's cancelled, kids. By 24,000 tons of projected
choking fumes. Nature rambles' studies gone. Play indoors,
windows locked '

MAJOR ERRORS

'Would-be racing-driver crashed himself, Ann's brother's
ashes now in Silverstone. Mad Car Disease crash,'
'Mad cow disease. Beef, bless him, Bill loved. Would-be
killer cancer drove him. Doctors… opinions
posing as facts.'
Toxic profit-making. Whale corpse 16 kilos of plastic inside.
Cash is king?
'Grandad, need to cry now...'

WELFARE?

'Outrage! Won't cocoon you in comfort blankets.
Ann, as a fledgling doctor, National Health Service opened.

Surgery had a queue round the block.
People after *free* cotton-wool.
Recycling medicine bottles - pah!
On my triple bypass, nurses insisted I had pain killers.
No pain I said, but pills were protocol!

Bankrupt!'

R.I.P-off BRITAIN

'Cheaper, dead. Coffin, in advance…'
'Sir, you homeless…'
'Cornflake-box. Leaks acid rain sommat rotten.
Drowning me…'
'Housing Benefits provide no coffins for residents. Sorry. '
'Waste of wood. Like me, redundant. Plastic instead.
Anyway, leaving body to nuclear research? Nirex?
Leastways, I'll go on living...thousands of years.
And active, Radio-active.'

RESURRECTIONS?

'Dead cobwebs, Ann. Hair's dead-fibre protean.
Grows in coffins, like toenails. Your dad shaved. '

'Step-mum said, "Worms get enough roughage!"'

'Dad also said, "Death doesn't exist,
Grandad. No destruction
…just waste…can't die…"'

'Like springtime. My grandson loved green. Now in astral
pastures of Self-development. Opportunities never stop…'

THE LAW

'Many sick teachers. 9 on permanent leave. Money's finished. Your school, Ann. Fancy home education? Legal, thank goodness. Yes, with me? State schools paid from an imaginary Money Tree. So, let's legalise cannabis. Put a heavy tax on it - Higher than nicotine!'
'Drunk teachers will resign, Grandad.' 'Have already!'

BABY-SITTING

'Ann with no 'e'. Yes, no artificial additives!'
'Also, we don't use disposable diapers. Problem?'
'500 nappies destroy one tree - and you've got triplets. No room thermostats or low-energy lightbulbs.
Synthetic fabrics on their cots, false flowers…'
'You want this job or not? We pay well!'
'Ecology matter.'
'Smug brat!'

ALL GREEK?

'Why deliver lessons' gifts in boxes. Life doesn't...'
'Boxing Day, Grandad!'
'You a boy I'd box your ears! Joking! Specialization good? Bad as Sophists bringing *sophistication*, to all but Peter Pan. And you, Ann. Convinced Pantheist bodies of knowledge. Comprehension comes through what…?'
'Slaughter!'
'Cosmic death-wish follows Law of Attraction!'

ASH CASH

'8 of 10 shopkeepers illegally sold Ann fags making
millions. Shouldn't tobacco companies sponsor cancer
research, not sport? Greg laughs at all deaths. '
'You're into football, Ann. Aiming for the
World Cup. So why smoke?
A tall girl hunk like you. Why?'

'Guess fear of feeling too small, Ann.'

UNSEEN

Landlubbers view no coral's fairy fish frisk
Can't therefore accept ecological risk
Rate relentless as rain wilful as weathervane
Lousy as lice irrepressible as mice
Less lasting than Lovers' Lane
Mammoth fossil prints on Wight
Peat bogs to cotton grass fatalism is a farce
Serving as sunlight optimism feels right?

NATURE'S PALLETS

'Art, Ann, seeing inwardly. Kirlian photography reveals a
multi-coloured halo around all living tissue. Fingertips
change hues with every thought, every snack.'
'Raw anger, like untaxed meat, Grandad? Green for mental
peace?' 'Chameleons, cuttlefish, artists absorbing the
colour of their surrounds. Camouflage.' See inner
LIGHT...? Yes?'

CARDBOARD CITIES

'Wisdom don't need no paper qualifications. Comic
cut-outs, us…' growls lager lout. 'Only me lice ain't
'omeles.'

'Addictive, attitude,' added failed businessman, smoking
sawdust.
Scratching scabies, Jack spews scraps scraped from
wastebins, splattering lavatory bucket, left begging to
shocked commuters…
'Bit life, like this sick-bucket…
No hobo wants to kick…?'

WARNING

'Tallest Hopi carved a kiss on the second tallest tree,
Grandad!'
'Canoes needed.'
'Tree nearest his tepee to all the forest whispered,
"AXEMAN!"'

'The tallest Hopi and the tallest tree met next dawn.
In a dead faint…
The tree fell.
Ann closed her book. 'Pity.
But I like reading books.'

FRIENDS IN NEED

Having survived deep in a flooded coal-mine,
man and rat on a raft.
Ocean breakers battered, relentlessly.
Both animals stared, starving, afraid to breathe.
9 shores they reached. Lands contaminated by wars…
Nearly dead, man and rat were rescued.
Safe?
Terrified, the rat jumped ship, drowned. The
rescued man cried

COMMUNICATIONS

18-months-old babbling babes can make every sound in the
universe, uniting birds, beasts and unseen beings in
understanding
Their purpose. In service.

As Babel grew taller, the tower like all life,
reached towards heaven.
Speaking in forked-tongues, God's imposters cursed Babel's
rampant diversity. Tower collapsed. Is Esperanto newly
refined Babel?

MEGALOPOLIS?

Below canopies of kelp fronds, candelabras of sponges,
sea-anemones, fishlike flower faces and multi-coloured
shoals, all swarming in restful oceanic rock-gardens off New
England's coastline. Cradled in sun-blessed undulations,
swaying lobster larvae
Beneath, cavernous sea-nurseries, teeming with organisms,
a well-ordered watery wilderness of photosynthesizing
plants.

Situated there,
An offshore oil-terminal?

SEE NO EVIL

3 remaining monkeys climb the one remaining tree…
3 remaining leaves fall...following the last 3
drops of acid rain…

3 remaining birds cough, as through black syrup air they
flap...seeking a green tree as hundreds
of burrowing beetles hide.

While dying monkeys weakly wave,
beetles keep on burrowing…

COLOUR BLIND

Again, the volcano spewed.
Dignitaries and all mankind, brown, red, yellow, black and white frazzled under fiery lava, without the royal family on their yacht.

As dust thinned, old games had to change. Not chess. By mixing colours the interbred dun race lived on kissing through with

Masked mouths

Checkmate?

ECONOMIC TEASERS

Who makes most money, supermarkets, dictators or The Royal Mint?
Who makes least, the unemployed or the beggar?
Who saves most, war babies, banks or new emotive church ministers? If every leaf on every tree was worth an expensive green note of money, might all breathe more easily in bed?

LOOSE CHANGE?

One world cryptocurrency for digital control.
Denomination domination, an abomination? Fluid clouds,
hackable machines. Since 2009, 4,000 variants have been
created risking virtual bankruptcy. Strangulating growing
poor populations. Free markets going slowly mad unseen.
Any ever authenticated by wary banks? Golden Mean,
labour...?
For ancient Mullahs, financial exploitation immoral.
Barter?

SENSITIVITY

Plants talking back in classrooms are they accused of cheek?
Who tells gardeners when to plant? What if the moon could
speak?
Live brine shrimp dropped in hot water disturbing their
vegetable dream, SCREAM"
Repeated when dead, nearby shrimps not now perturbing
their Living team
Cut grass makes moaning lawns?

NATURE'S GNOSIS

Soft pink and open like vagina as all life
the lotus is a climber
From mud towards Light, chakras hidden from sight.
Do jungles practice Feng-Shui
Landscape shapes suggest chi flows
Female ground emits unheard soundwaves
For greenery growing
5 planets and Chinese elements linked
As if life hides knowing?

CURRENTS

Wind and water intermediaries between Heaven and earth.
Water our great life sustainer, evaporation each
raindrops rebirth
Winds of change not always keeping us saner
Until we learn energy's secrets divine
At winter weather in spring folks will whine
Not placing at home, a benign wind-chime to say, 'Life's
Sublime!'

ATTITUDES

Gentle winds bring contentment. Unanswered
prayers resentment
Change placement of mirrors and beds?
As if unreal symbolically thinking aspirin
takes pains from heads
False beliefs won't remove certain facts. Pax?
If we think global decline is certain, pessimism can draw
the final curtain, expecting no encores
closing tight all doors.

HOLLOW EARTH?

An Arctic animal stuffing tropical food, Mammoths' mouths
with undigested shoots of pine. Earth a peopled planet
early understandings crude. Overheated gasses as planets
solidly refine from nebula acquiring a hollow inside where
interplanetary refugees hide avoiding terminal decline,
warmed by an interior sun generating sustenance.
Continental drift again re-define…?

HOLY MOLY

Like defunct dodos Indian herds of beef
Their threatened lives rendered brief
Holiest Brahmin requested guidance received
Before the last wet-nurse milking mother grieved
A sacred edict promoted them to Holy Cow

Future dairy slaughter breaking a God-given vow
Not all other species profane those on earth not here now.

MONTHLY HOLYDAYS

Sunlit simple molecules obeying unseen rules
Invisible as imagination
Lightwaves carrying energetic information
Allowed creations to read and adapt to conditions
As with axis again shifting before earth flips
So best read ecologists' lips.
Deprived contact with countrysides changing conditions
Modern city folk need a regular rural break as remission.

GENESIS

A master organiser of a Masterly Plan
Affecting efficient growth of both beast and man.
DNA explanations deficient? Atheism insufficient?
Scientifically blinded flies produce strains of sightless eyes
Until a compensating gene as white knight
Miraculously restores former sight.
No Lord of the Flies can afford to rival Life's LORD?

COSMIC CLASSROOMS

Powerbases hide implicit blackmail
Making victims comply and quail feeling
their own powers will fail
State education seek compliance, aiming for
subjects total reliance
Swelling power-brokers' coffers while
Nature gives free offers
Unemotional provisions we making our revisions
Its lessons as blessings to share, we deciding
which shoes to wear.

BROADENS THE MIND

Traveling days bring pages of education
Outreach engaging each ambitious nation
Notions Victorians savoured oceans
challenge with Sky-high seawaves
Empire explorers' excursions preferred
Some bones left in cannibals' graves
Pillaged plants from Himalayan Heights
Giant colourful butterflies flowers dazzling strange sights
Do the godless lack gratitude for
cynical downsized attitude?

DESALINATION

Problems walk themselves for those who walk with elves
Enjoying tranquil rural release
Watching changing seasons seeking mental peace.
Green apples picked too soon ripeness
no man can dragoon
The reddest at sundrenched tree's crown
As Arab olive trees invaders pulled down
Land colonised with seawater turned into a lagoon.

HELP!

Being willing is to be able
Positive thinking on your table
If you can conceive it you can achieve it
Cleaning up beaches dirty streets delittered
Help save the planet less embittered. Daily
affirmations at dawn.
To aid modes of healthy reform
Is saying YES to life reduces emotional strife.

MUTUALLY ASSURED?

Instead of winging about what's wrong be
grateful for what's right
Only sing a happy song do-gooding needs love not a fight
Each weapon system nature's first, acid in
chemical warfare burst
Defence BOOMerangs cost the earth dear.

Human love conquered by indoctrinated fear?

State-bribed students to status quo adhere?

STEPPING-STONES

One star can't make a constellation
Nature's generosity causes contention
Mean-minded folk trapped in their yoke
Wild animals aching to be freed from cages
Impatient maybe to return as Sages.
Those not earthbound rate Nature's not profound
A passing illusion won't bow to delusion
Spirit and matter adders of fusion

SELF-LOVE?

Victims feeling unloved threaten environments
Never enjoying summer flower gardens' perfumes.
Write Mother Nature a love letter,
Not long till you feel better
Love and creativity linked at the hip
Don't be wary. Alternatives scary
Only rats decide to jump ship.
Peacocks like lions, love sunbathing, in shade they kip.

BALANCING LOBES

People who don't break things never create anything -
Filipino proverb; Philippines plagued by typhoons,
landslides earthquakes, tsunamis, floods.
Islanders floundering in corrupted muds…
Reminiscent of ancient lands of Atlantis and Mu
Now as legends were always untrue.
Brains need fables as in WATCH THE BIRDIES book. Now
take a look?

READING SIGNALS

Those not ruled by rudders ruled by rocks - Welsh saying.

After hearing drowning sea captains praying?
Consult Leonardo's drawings of manes of horses and
watercourses
Not from mains. Rapids can be rabid consumers.
River's negative 'secret arrows' as rumours point to V or Y
Grave black spots dangers luring strangers.

DISCARDING?

Throw-away clothes waste incredible
Takeaways' litter inedible
For seagulls and pigs no dates with strange figs
As Brexit both sides unbiddable
World Cup coated with plastic dolphins
and fish mad spastic
Litter cleared by black fans from abroad
Zulu brides' silk gowns can't afford
Robed in rubbish loved litter glowing!

CRIES

If something to say, say it! - Anonymous proverb.

Protests unheard can cause indigestion
Violent protests maybe best to question
Like harming a distant relative too close
Litter-clearing should not include corpses.
Which more earth-friendly, burial or cremation;
Ashes sprinkled on sea or land. Back to
dust as God's planned.

INGRATITUDE?

Eating a fruit, thank the person who planted the tree –
Vietnamese proverb.

Imagine multinational supermarkets buyers
Dismissing ugly fruit saying this from the heart. Gratitude is
always a good start to all engagements with pressing
matters.
So easy to scold but saying please can feel hot
While 'thankyou' somewhat cold?

WHY DELAY?

Sleepy turtles never catch up with the sunrise - Jamaican saying.

The moment, use it or lose it? Sleepwalkers
on autopilot, time now to wake-up? No
problem or accepted challenge?
Well begun is half done if prevaricating?
On addressing ecological reviews?
Time and motion discipline
Might save sea rises nearest you.

APATHY

May you live all the days of your life - Jonathan Swift.

Polluted air, life's more than breathing. Toxic food, life's more than eating and sleeping pills. Chemical warfare with pharmaceutical big
business guys, profiteering on ailments, banning healthy cheaper and effective herbs and potions.
Too disillusioned? Obedience - expedience?

THE POWER OF NOW

To thine own self be true - Shakespeare on Hamlet's uncertainty,
The Prince an everyman?

Like you, your family, even teachers…Preachers.
The louder the voice, they laud hollow core beliefs?
Given you *are* Soul, how many selves *have* you?
Your nature on the way to Supernature/Natural?
The Readiness is ALL!

ENTROPY?

Our sun/son male/yang and moon female/yin;
That is, including Mother Nature
Those who say all physical life is but an
illusion, are they mistaken?
Is Fair Trade unreal, like Garden of Eden, if not everlasting?
How epic the BIG Picture, our expanding cosmos
One
Orgasmic
BIG
BANG?

DOGMATIC DIETS?

Gram by gram a loaf; stone by stone a castle - Yugoslav proverb.

Wisdom's whole - lies true. They exist! Yet temporary like all
physicality, not permanent reality. The food-chain love's
evolutionary ladder. No fear of death above.
Mankind aware of morality.
Cows scenting slaughtered sisters, tremble.

Meat-eaters eat more healthy vegetarians.

DREAMS MANIFEST

Believing something impossible makes it true. Being willing is enabling - French proverbs.

Use visualization as the Law of Attraction. Your power more than a fraction. Thought precedes action. Belief trumps all. If this in doubt, ask Mr Trump of Trump Tower. To be willing is empowering.
Disbelief deflowering.
Deforesting devastating

MULTI-EVERYTHING

Bad ploughmen quarrel with his ox - Korean proverb.

Astrological earth signs are three; Capricorn - Duchess of Cambridge; Elvis Presley, late developer. Taurus - beauty lover; Adele, George Clooney. Vigo - into tiny details. Elizabeth 2, Queen of England, Prince Harry.
Celebrate many types of soil, plants, animals, people,
Insects, planets, cultures,
Civilizations.

THE MUSHROOM MEN

Don't borrow another's nose to breathe with - Thai saying.

Dismiss your passions, embrace your 6 senses, including
your gut's brain. Make intuition your guide
Brave pacifist Quaker Friends have the deserved reputation
For protesting against all military clout.
Hurting the state GDP more dangerous
Than stumbling blindly to nuclear burn-out?

HONORABLE HARI-KARI?

1 arrow is easily snapped, a quiver-full, not - Japanese saying.
Bags of Easter eggs, bagfuls of H-Bombs? In the Gobi
Desert, 4 layers down, archaeologists no head in the sand,
found greenish glass-like sand covering vast square-miles.
Nuclear desert for afters?
Despite Hiroshima nuclear power stations leaks
into Japanese waters.

FAIR TRADE

If the shoe fits wear it - English saying.

Who'd rather wear-out than retire?
Commercial obsolescence built-in like car's toxic exhaust,
Clean as a bean!
Where the wealthy who never told a lie?
As if all deeds not accountable, no problem insurmountable
When fairness a law,
Mankind rejecting tooth and claw?

PROGRESS?

When the solution is simple, God is answering - Albert Einstein,
the teacher's feared dunce. 'Stand in the corner at once!'
After paradise lost left in mother's womb, on earth, with
shrinking room and resources, fearful nations boost their
forces.

As crocuses push through concrete...
Creation's incomplete…?

WISDOM'S WAY?

Avoid extremes O monks. Take the Middle Way - the Buddha.
Centre roads less worn.

The Natural World colonizers ghost cities' dead
manufacturing headquarters. Anyone miss railway porters
As folk carry their own loads?
Compromise not nature's way,
Safety in numbers saving the day.
With no spine, life supine. Not sublime?

PERSISTENCE

If at first you don't succeed, try, try again - English saying.

Perseverance pays, unlike lazy delays. Mankind's birthright,
as stewards of the earth

Breaking bad repeated patterns, the secret need for rebirth.
Hence the spring when songbirds sing and lambs leap
Honeybears leave sleep.
Steady application improves ecology's healing
medication…?

ALL ROADS CIRCULAR…?

Don't soldier ants bury their dead, elephants trumpet
funerals…?

Is a two-way mirrored swing-door dead - collie two lives back
Was same owner's cat-on-the-bed
Both knew it, new dog leading to the food cupboard a sign
Using same paw to clean his face as when feline.
All lives plus 9?

BARDO!

Pliny dictated cool descriptions. Investigating, he sailed to death,
He buried with Naples by Vesuvius ash. Now an archaeologist
Whose inner truth hones, excavating his own last bones?
Which doctor regressing patients wrote embodied Souls chosen
Lives before *Lives*?
Aberfan slagheap smothering schoolkids many predicted but prevention methods remain conflicted.

PROPORTIONATE

A shapely tree egg-timer and chalice
Well-proportioned like a palace
Balance conceivable owned as believable
Harmonies harbour no malice
Covering all life, the law of action and reaction, CAUSE and effect:
Through proud minds will deflect Divinity will detect every small defect and nothing neglect. All is love elect.

IDENTITY PARADE

12 suspects enter the greenhouse, watchful trees present
12 stately witnesses wired-up, witnessing assassin's axe split
Gardener's skull on a green agitator's cull

As this murderer returns, these tropical witnesses shake...
Sap squeals...our lie-detectors alerted
12 trees good and true, judge
12 suspects, one by one, checked…
Justice not averted.

CLAIRVOYANT

Weeping vicar, with Babel head, appeared
at ground-floor flat
By world-famous Direct Voice Medium greeted
'Sorry, Your Reverend, dogs not allowed.'
The Pastor suffering two fatalities; his teen
son's motorbike boast
Had slaughtered family's Labrador
Before fatally crashing into their home's front door

Through many walls Medium sent canine's ghost.

NO DOMINION

Dead pampered poodles, over-cosseted cats
Trussed-up in Sunday attire. From earth
they temporarily retire
Animal coffins supplied, velvet interior, no creature inferior

An animal communicating Celebrant announces that
Prajapati
An Indian Master is dancing with both pets on a
Happy Hunting Party
Before returning roles rehearsed,
Sexes and species, reversed.

OVERKILL

An Arab Prince so relished shooting unarmed gamebirds
he ordered Scottish pheasant eggs.

Back in his own kingdom he waited impatiently for his
plane to deliver like a mother hen. When the prize eggs
were unpacked, they'd hatched.

Jumping with excitement he shot all the chicks dead.

OVER-POPULATED?

No cardboard-boxes hordes sleeping on pavements, no silk sheets, littering streets.
Flaunting sweetmeats criminals groomed hobos into gun-lobbies.
Uneaten fur-coated foxes faring better,
Crying orphans clogged uncounted regular begging,
Tourists stopped buying. Vigilante shopkeepers arming-up, hired scruffy hitmen. One by one, as they stole hotel scraps,
Skinny kids killed.

SNAKES AND…?

Souls queuing-up for Planet Earth gatecrashers claim time for rebirth.
Their last chance saloon to Love's Laws re-tune, of vacant wombs still no dearth.
Jacob's ladder he climbed when first young, starting at the bottom rung, many times over, his life seeking clover.
To beat them best, lessons then blest.

REDHANDED?

As football and fishing compete, one offering active power,
second-hand Other anglers with biggest catches,
grandstand
Measuring their items like schoolboys behind bike-sheds
Mutual interest hooked.

Fish, like books, like financial audits, can be cooked.
But do fish suffer, squirming, lips oozing, life slowing losing
After fish-and-chips fishermen boozing?

CADETS?

Distrusting kids' innate goodwill as silence
schoolteachers instil?
Afraid of riots, barked too loud, 'Be QUIET!'
Old Testament's 'Do as I will! - or else!'
Best to scare the circus beasts?
No longer lawful captive classroom pests
After facing tests Childhood dreams fade in forced regimes,
Profits before people infest/invest?

HEDGE FUNDS

Fearing their own power will fail,
Every powerbase by implicit blackmail
Makes its sad victims comply and to quail
Hence education seeks compliance to gain
its subjects total reliance
To swell its offers, while nature has free unsolicited offers
Healthy provisions to share as we decide
which shoes to wear.

FREQUENCIES

Stonehenge and Oxfordshire's Rollright Stones
Druids used these ancient cosmic phones.

With crop-circles they can in Spirit cause elevation
Mind and body experiencing elation Solstice Celebrations
with dancing and singing Auschwitz birds staying silent
No toll-bells ringing, while wasps and nettles go on stinging
Dock leaves before potions relief bringing.

LAKE DISTRICT

New National World Heritage Vintage Site
Steam engines bring blight.
On water and land coal-fires, still not banned,
Plumes of smoke imprinting their might.

Trains on regular runs on rails here and abroad
While angry protester's voice fails unheard,
As if a fraud, profit-seekers not deterred
Conscience not yet stirred…?

REVERSES?

Every belief system riven; dogmas not seen God-given
Uncertainties overdue, sea tides rising not so new,
Can old dictators be forgiven?
Local larders all bare, life reckoned unfair, rich palaces spike air,
No gold left to share, generous poor not rare,
As vigilantes glare, laugh sing and dance – Don't dare!

EDUTAINMENT

While in forests ancient logs burn, Life
and nature's ways Listeners learn.
No books or paper, as fairy folk caper,
Storyteller each taking a turn.

Personal experiences more engaging than explanations;
Cliff-hangers with, nuclear explosion coastal erosion, folk
on the edge, attention captured enraptured, with 'dangers'

Aphrodisiac no amnesiac

SUGARY GRANDAD

'I could give you a hundred pounds a week Ann, but
wouldn't it be better to earn it? Well, what do you think girl,
all giving and no getting and then what
happens to aged me…?'

'All grabbing, no giving what happens to *you, Grandad…?*
How should we spend
Our love?'

AN EYE FOR AN EYE

Every action has an equal and opposite reaction...so what price balances -...co-incidences, Rockefellers always rich, the poor always with us…? For every 'present' there's an opposite and equal sequel. Every turn, a re-turn...every lessen re-cognition…? Poor sight for rich optician... sweet-rotten teeth for rich dentists?
Choices…chances…rejoices?

TRANSIENCE

30 million types
Of animals
And plants
Thoroughbreds and hybrid
ALL interlinked
Consider how different your uncles and aunts?
What can link them, but shared consciousness synced?
Each on a ladder of learning
As globe and seasons keep churning.
Alert with hope how best to cope
On evolution's slippery slope…?

ADAM-OLUTION - 1 -

Mind's radio on all frequencies set
Uses brain's brawn its chemistry net.
When God was dead, men lost their reigns
Alive God's love not hard corn but grains
To cook for others, all sisters, all brothers
Shrinking at last most binary pains.
Let intuition re-mind the intellect
Ever-present God loves every sect

ADAM- OLUTION - 2 -

That telepathy preceded the telephone future rich religions
Soul must hone. The Word on Winds inflating human flesh
As lateral longings become mere literal
Creation's Monoblock split cock from clitoral.
Eden's lost paradise our incestuous crèche.
Hides with two tits, two lobes, two legs,
Ripening up
Their multitudes of eggs.

ADAM–OLUTION - 3 -

From East to West, South to Northern Pole
Two minds bipolar sensing one Whole.
Stewards of Earth Seas and Skies
Forgetting eternity as fleet time flies
Upon earth seeking the seesaw's safe centre
Healed by the Self, Soul's l/only sole Mentor
Ready to greet and radiantly re-meet
Our alchemical Inventor?

EVE-OLUTION - 1 -

Sacred Serpent your sibilant hiss
Whispers paradise must lose its bliss.
Fruit provided on fig-leaf plates I and Adam need Altered States
Not besotted with ripest fruit
But learn love as lamb and brute.
Adam stays deaf to my need to talk
Kills me with kisses speaks of the Stork

EVE-OLTION - 2 -

Adam sees my love weak, my body his right
We spawning boys to swear and fight
Crushing their sisters grabbing fattest apples,
I so feel far from smart –
With visions and voices my mind still grapples
Pronounced unreal by males into power.
Oh Serpent, help my honey not turn sour.

EVE-OLITION - 3 -

Husbands and wives, kith and kin.
You say centuries of yang and yin
Will teach us the virtues of sin.

Just as soon as we no longer seek to win.
This waxing world and its leaden ways –

Then not too wilful to begin
Return our inner ways to holy praise

EVE-OLUTION - 4 -

Two tribes spit swearwords blaming others
Named bullets fatally maiming brothers
All weapons seem strong, all missing what's wrong

Black Dog Days whelps not whipped
Rover lost his pack.
Will his master come back knowing he wept?
Depression going as in foetus curl, he slept?
Open one eye perfectly dry.

EVE-OLUTION - 5 -

If all cows not eaten global warming beaten
Less cows expiring less cars backfiring
Cut off bulls' balls like we're Cretan?

If Darwin's theory all revered
Why don't all monkeys grow a beard?

Watch granny grin as kittens suckle her hairy chin
Result of the way by their queens reared?

EARTHY LINKS

Thin green snake?
Slowly swaying from side-to-side seeking a safe place to hide,
to thrive and to feed; to flourish and to seed, its life
flowering to full, the best actions existential and essential
for further foods.
Depending on local weather's moods.

Not a serpent seen but a bramble sapling

SOVERIGN RESOURCES

(Taken from Dovetales Godly Geography)

From Amazon's hard grained woods to green Robin bootie,
Dinosaurs' and dodos' beauty,
Dead tusks and tigers, toxic lead,
Robbing others' goods, animals and land.
Was that the Way the gods unmanned Mars, Moon and
Gobi's Desert Sand?
Earth' rare creatures, indispensable?
For good Earth's kindly folks, incomprehensible and
reprehensible.

HOW FAST IS A SLOW DEATH?

(Taken from my Dovetales Godly Geography)

Half a million verges in GB Sport wildflowers to
feed the bee.
How many million miles of tar entomb earthworms to free
the car… Woodlands left for killing blood sports?
Oil-tankers to choke up smelly ports?
How many hamburgers with B.S.E
Before God's milk and honey avoid final tragedy…?

RICH SEASONS

As rain on spring soil stirs seeds from winter's sleep
So rest from human toil like spring lambs will leap.
Sunshine fled from summer sky Uncomplaining flora dry,
Busy Pisky flower-fairies frisky,
Full-blown each bloom
Till hidden worlds' ethereal lights outshine
Autumn's coloured palette. Inner Light
The most sublime.

BUSY BUZZERS

Bees buzzing fruit fatter fertilising before they scatter
Apples and pears, helping world's affairs, even if costing purse more
Our lives longer than before.
Plant blooms along each road
Countering chemicals on overload.
Specs sitting on the end of noses,
Help us smell not just success but also roses.

SUCKERS?

Ivy hugs all trees in sight with selfish might, tenacious her love-bites. Serious call for woodland therapy - right? Bloated foliage hurricanes' delight as trees become a kite.

Ivy apes bindweed but without wedding white blooms.
Catch suffocating plants advertising for more rooms?
No parasites, no Dutch girl with ear-studded pearl

EVERY BODY

Everybody can rescue whatever each chooses.
A frog alive or red mid-road mince?
God's love never loses, not one pauper not one prince.
Providence in each sparrow's fall
For a sparrowhawk never too small to ferociously maul.
May man and wife both learn to say -

'LET'S SAVE ALL LIFE'
NOW!'

ANIMAL TESTING?

Snatched from mum content in her forest tree
Chimpanzees injected with HIV
Food poked through bars, collecting scars
Scientists will cut such beastly cruelty…?
Not robots.
Our cousins are God's creatures, incarcerated,
Outraged, jailed screechers, pains ignored, cures explored,
Victims always humanity's teachers.
Now in Chimp Haven, no longer craven.

PRIORITIES

On Shangrila's lowlands fertile fields' floods
reach far. Farm food
Refined, processed foods folks don't mind
Feeding health-giving whole-meal millet
to their budgerigar!
Traditional happy birthday iced sponge cake
Engraved messages part of its make
No biases bleat from those who eat meat,
Prejudiced people don't make a loving cake?
Author Christopher Gilmore offers a new musical called
SHANGRILA!

BIO-DIVERSITIES

85% coral reefs left cleansing endangered
oysters and plankton
Due to over-exploitation by Pacific traders until suchlike
Populated self-sustaining sea-beds, dead.
Contrasting with interconnected diversity, the Brazil nut's
flower is only fertilized by one species of bumblebee, wind-
fallen nuts partially chewed, rest buried by squirrel-type
agoutis seeding clusters of trees.

BULLISH

Most species of lemur at risk In Madagascar
Many eaten or trapped as illegal mild pets
Transported far.
Not that Machiavellian plotting is unknown amongst chips
Arguably man's nearest ancestor, relatively? Not imps
Being green not easy for wrestling male bullfrogs in mating time
With
L o n g l e g s Hiding In
Bogs.

FROG IN HER THROAT

FROG IN HER THROAT

FROGGIE WAS SAD. HE WANTED A TAIL. A TAIL LIKE A BIRD.
WHY WAS THAT?
BECAUSE HE WANTED TO FLY...FLY AS HIGH AS A BIRD…BUT
NO TAIL AND NO…?
NO WINGS, YES. NO WINGS.
BUT HE DID HAVE SOMETHING ELSE.
WHAT MIGHT THAT BE?
HE COULD JUMP…BUT HE ALSO HAD A WISH...
TO JUMP HIGHER THAN ALL THE OTHER FROGS.
AND SOMETHING ELSE HE HAD DO ALSO....

GUESS WHAT ELSE HE HAD?

HE HAD ANOTHER SORT OF TALE.
NOT THE TYPE THAT CAN WAG LIKE A DOG.
NOT THE TYPE THAT CAN WAVE LIKE A CAT THAT'S CROSS
BUT A MAGIC TAIL...A STORY…
LIKE TO HEAR FROGGIE'S STORY?
HE'D BE SO HAPPY BECAUSE...WELL, THAT'S A SECRET.
MAYBE YOU'LL GUESS.
AND MAYBE YOU'LL FIND OUT LATER WHEN YOU LISTEN
LISTEN TO FROGGIE'S SECRET TALE.
DO YOU LIKE SECRETS?

READY…?

MANY YEARS AGO, BEFORE FROGGIE WAS BORN,
A STRANGE PRINCESS LIVED.
THE PRINCESS LOVED SINGING

TO THE BIRDS AND THE BEES
WITH NO WORDS
TO SILENT TREES...AND HUG THEM TIGHT IN CASE
SOME HORRID PERSON WANTED TO CHOP THEM
DOWN.
PLEASE, NOT HER FAVOURITE APPLE TREE.

BUT OFTEN SHE FELT TIRED…

…SO TIRED THAT SHE YAWNED
YAWNED IN THE MIDDLE OF A SONG
YAWNED VERY LOUDLY
SO LOUDLY THAT THE KING HER FATHER GOT…
GOT WHAT…?
YES, VERY ANGRY. CROSS.
SO CROSS, HE GROWLED LIKE DOG,
BUT STILL THE PRINCESS YAWNED
EVEN LOUDER
"USE YOUR HAND!" SHOUTED THE KING
"OVER YOU MOUTH. LIKE THIS…"

BUT PRINCESS PECULIAR WOULD NOT.
SHE LOVED BEING NAUGHTY.
SO KNOW WHAT SHE DID DO…?
SHE KEPT HER MOUTH…?
O P E N
SO O P E N YOU COULD SEE INSIDE
ALL THE APPLE JELLY SHE LOVED TO EAT.YUK!
WORSE!
AT SUPPER TIME
SHE ATE EVEN MORE RED JELLY…
WITH HER MOUTH GAPING WIDE O P E N!
THAT HAD THE KING SHOUTING...WHAT…?

AGAIN SHOUTING
"CLOSE OUR MOUTH GIRL!"
PRINCESS PECULIA SHRUGGED

SHRUGGED HER SHOULDERS
AND SAID
GUESS WHAT SHE SAID…
SHE SAID, "DADDY, IF I KEEP MY MOUTH SHUT, THEN
WHAT…?"

VERY ANGRY NOW WAS HE.
NOT THE QUEEN, NOT SHE,
SHE KEEP HER MOUTH SHUT IN CASE OF...WELL,
SHUT ANYWAY
THEY REALLY BOTH LOVED THEIR PECULIAR
DAUGHTER.
NOW THE PRINCESS WAS ALSO ANGRY.

"I'LL STARVE TO DEATH, THAT'S WHAT…
THAT'S WHAT I'LL DO, WITH NO APPLE JELLY INSIDE
ME -
SO THERE!" "GO TO YOUR ROOM!"
THE KING POINTED WAY UP HIGH
"GO TO YOUR ROOM NOW!" PRINCESS PECULIAR
RAN….
RAN VERY FAST
OUT OF THE PALACE
EVER FASTER
SO FAST HER MOUTH OPEN UNTIL....WHAT…?
A LOUD VOICE... IN HER HEAD...SAID..."STOP!"
STOP SHE DID. AND STARED. MOUTH OPEN...
AMAZED.
GUESS WHAT SHE SAW...?

SHE SAW A FROG...A BEAUTIFUL GREEN FROG
WHAT IS HIS NAME? YES, IT'S OUR FRIEND FROGGIE.
WHAT HAPPENED NEXT?
THE PRINCESS WANTED TO KNOW WHAT HAPPENED
NEXT,
DO YOU…?

WELL, ALL HAD A GOOD GUESS? LOVELY! THAT MEANS
YOU ALL GOT SUCH GOOD FRIENDS.
NOT FROGGIE
HE HAD NOT ONE FRIEND
BECAUSE…?
HE LIKED LEAPING
LEAPING LIKE A SPRING LAMB...ON SPRINGS…
LEAPING UP TO HIS LEFT
UP TO HIS RIGHT
EACH TIME GETTING HIGHER
HIGHER THAN THE LAST JUMP.
THAT WAS WHY FROGGIE HAD NO FRIENDS
THAT WAS WHY FOR FROGGIE WITH NO GARDEN PONDS
NO WATER TO SPLASH IN!

AND NOT ONE FRIEND
TO PLAY JUMPING GAMES WITH…
NO OTHER FROGGIE FRIEND.
BECAUSE…?
BECAUSE HE COULD JUMP HIGHER THAN ALL OTHER FROGS.
GUESS WHY OTHER FRIENDS DIDN'T' LIKE HIM…?
BECAUSE…?
YES, HE COULD FLY AS HIGH AS A BABY BIRD.
BUT BACK DOWN ON EARTH AGAIN
FROGGIE WOULD WEEP…. FROGGIE WOULD CRY
BIG FROGGIE TEARS
TEARS IN HIS LEFT EYE...TEARS IN HIS RIGHT EYE...
BOO-HOO BOO-HOO! BOO-HOO BOO-HOO!
WHY DID FROGGIE CRY…? BECAUSE…?
BECAUSE HE HAD NO FRIENDS...ALL ALONE...ALL BY HIMSELF
UNTIL…UNTIL...UNTIL SUDDENLY HE SAW…
WHO…?

YES! PRINCESS PECULIAR...HER MOUTH WIDE
OPEN…
AND STRAIGHT AWAY SHE STOPPED CRYING...NO
MORE TEARS.
SHE WAS AMAZED BY...
WHO WAS SHE AMAZED BY…?
WHY WAS PRINCESS PECULIA AMAZED…?
YES, HIS SKILL IN JUMPING...JUMPING SO VERY VERY
HIGH…

HAD FROGGIE MADE A NICE NEW FRIEND…?
FROGGIE WANTED TO KNOW...WANTED TO KNOW…
WHAT?

YES. WHAT WOULD HAPPEN NEXT?
DO YOU...WANT TO KNOW WHAT WOULD HAPPEN
NEXT?
YES…?
GOOD! VERY VERY GOOD…!

THEN HAVE A CHAT
AND HAVE A GOOD GUESS
ALL OF YOU

TOGETHER.

SO GLAD WAS FROGGIE TO HAVE A NEW FRIEND
THAT HE JUMPED FOR JOY!
HE JUMPED TO HIS LEFT…. JUMPED TO HIS RIGHT…
ALWAYS HIGHER AND HIGHER
BUT BEST OF ALL, HE JUMPED STRAIGHT UP...HIGH...
…HIGHER… HIGHEST OF ALL…
AND LANDED...WHERE...?

IN THE O P E N MOUTH OF WHO…? YES, PRINCESS
PRECULIA, YES!
NOW THEY BOTH WANTED TO KNOW...WHAT…"

WHAT WOULD HAPPEN NEXT
DO YOU? ARE YOU SURE…? REALLY SURE…? ME TOO!
…
SO SOMEONE PLEASE SUGGEST WHAT HAPPENS
NEXT?
REMEMBER PRINCESS PECULIA NOW HAS A LIVE
FROG IN HER
WIDE O P E N MOUTH…
SUGGESTIONS…?

OR SHALL I TELL YOU?
WELL, THE PRINCESS CLUTCHED HER THROAT
FIRST WITH HER LEFT HAND...THEN WITH HER
RIGHT HAND
THEN SHE PINCHED HER NOSE LIKE THIS…
FIRST WITH HER RIGHT HAND...THEN WITH HER
LEFT HAND.
THEN SHE CLOSED HER EYES...FIRST LEFT HER EYE...
THEN HER RIGHT EYE
AND STILL SHE DARE NOT SPEAK
NOT WITH A FROG IN HER THROAT.

NOTHING FOR IT BUT TO GO TO SLEEP.
IN SLEEP SHE MIGHT GET A DREAM
AND THE DREAM MIGHT TELL HER WHAT TO DO.
BETTER STILL!
IN THE DREAM SHE MIGHT MEET A...A... WHO MIGHT
SHE MEET…?
A HANDSOME PRINCE
AND HE MIGHT TELL HER…? WHAT…?
TELL HER WHAT BEST TO DO...
YES, TO DO WHEN SHE WOKE UP BRILLIANT!
BUT SHE SNORED
SNORED SO LOUDLY
THAT FROGGIE WANTED TO…?
CLOSE HIS EARS. BUT HE COULDN'T. WHY…?

BECAUSE HE HAD NO EARS. SO HE COULD NOT
CLOSE HIS EARS
SO BE STILL COULD HEAR...COULD HEAR…
LOUD…SNORES.
SO LOUD HE HAD TO MAKE A JUMP FOR IT.
THIS HE DID.
FROGGIE LANDED ON HIS FEET
- SPLAT – JUST LIKE THAT!
AND THEN
PRINCESS PECULIAR WOKE UP...AND SAW…
ANOTHER FROG? NO. THE HANDSOME PRINCE?
NO. HE WAS HORRIBLE.
HIS HAIR WAS GREEN...HIS EYES WERE GREEN...
HIS CHEEKS WERE GREEN
AND HE SHOUTED, JUST LIKE
THE KING, PECULIAR'S FATHER.
WHAT DID HE SHOUT?
HE SHOUTED - "SHUT YOUR MOUTH GIRL! –
THEN I CAN LOVE YOU..."
DO YOU THINK SHE DID...CLOSE HER MOUTH?
NOT QUITE. SHE SPOKE.
SHE SAID, "YOU LOOK LIKE A... YES, A FROG,
HORRIBLE!"

THE PRINCE STARTED TO JUMP.
HE JUMPED TO HIS LEFT…HE JUMPED TO HIS RIGHT
HE JUMPED STRAIGHT UP HIGH ...SO HIGH…
HE LANDED IN A TREE...AN APPLE TREE, HER APPLE
TREE.
PRINCESS PECULIAR LOVED AN APPLE A DAY
SO, SHE BEGGED...SHE PLEADED...EVEN PRAYED
FOR HIM TO PICK HER A BIG RED JUICY APPLE
AND TO THROW IT...
WHERE…?
STRAIGHT INTO HER WIDE O P E N MOUTH…?
NO.

"CLOSE YOUR MOUTH GIRL - I'M NOT A DENTIST!!"
AND SHE DID. SHE CLOSED HER MOUTH.

SO, HE THREW DOWN THE APPLE
A BIG RED JUICY APPLE...HARD! RIGHT ON HER HEAD...
BANG!
AND SHE FAINTED - FELL FLAT ON THE FLOOR...
AS IF FAST ASLEEP. BUT NO SNORING.
WAS SHE STILL BREATHING...?
WANT TO FIND OUT?

SHE WAS SNORING. GOOD! STILL ALIVE!
AND DREAMING.
WHAT DO YOU THINK SHE WAS DREAMING OF...?
YES, SHE PICTURED HERSELF AS A PRINCESS
WITH LOVELY DAZZLING HAPPY SMILE.
SHE MADE UP HER OWN MIND.
SHE DECIDED THAT WAS THE WAY TO LIVE
WHEN SHE WOKE UP.
AWAYS HAPPY.NEVER SNAPPY.
SMILING ALL THE TIME...JUMPING...JUMPING FOR JOY
FIRST TO HER RIGHT...THEN TO HER LEFT...
THEN EVER HIGHER.... AND... HIGHER...
AND HIGHER STILL TILL...
WELL, THAT'S HER SECRET NOW.
CAN YOU NOW GUESS WHO OR WHAT SHE SAW?

LET'S LEAVE HER ASLEEP SHALL WE. SLEEPING PEACEFULLY?
AND WHO KNOWS...WHEN SHE WAKES UP
SHE MIGHT SEE BESIDE HER...?
HER FATHER THE KING...WITH THE QUEEN...
BOTH OF HER LOVING PARENTS TOGETHER.
YES, THERE AT EITHER SIDE GENTLY CUDLING HER
SO PLEASED...SO VERY PLEASED BECAUSE...?

BECAUSE HER MOUTH WAS CLOSED. SHUT!
AND PRINCESS THEIR DAUGHTER WAS SAFE
SAFE AND SOUND ASLEEP STILL DREAMING....
DREAMING. DREAMING...
LET'S NOT WAKE HER...
SHHHH!

POSTERITY? - 1 -

A fly by night, prairie dog by day, we all can save whatever
We wish. The tiger moth, or rare angelfish,
What chef will revive a rare endangered dish?

Can an ant become an antelope, a Plantagenet a plant?
A cow a coward in a slaughterhouse
Regressing to a mouse?

POSTERITY? - 2 -

From tigerlily to little lamb, butterflies to Uncle Sam,
A million forms of life to choose,
From Adam's Eve to owls and shrews,
From fish to fowl, from ape to man,
Conservation the Master Plan.

Can an ant avoid an angry anteater?
A million seeds produce one Ann or Peter!

POSTERITY? - 3 -

Less wielding of butcher's bloody knife Everybody can
rescue whatever each chooses
Frogs alive or red roadside mince?
Every pauper, every prince
Crested newts or jars of outdated jam.

Each catastrophe and cat their nine lives not a scam

May man and wife both repeatedly say, 'LET'S SAVE ALL
LIFE'

POSTERITY? - 4 -

Archaeologists excavate their monkey bones unrecognised.
Archivists find their own ancient records personally prized.
Cats and dogs parrots and caged rabbits
Seek old keepers to repeat their pet family's habits?

'For God's love never loses as the hawk turns into the dove
Lacking limits Ann, all levels of energized love.'

HAZY HABITS

'Tell that boyfriend, Ann, 16 excuses for pot-smoking
18 for alcohol addiction. Passive smoking?
Worse than alcoholics driving? Drop him...'

'Grandad, we've given up giving up!'
'Study the statistics.
Dozens of doctors and youngsters kill themselves. 441 died
of lung cancer!'

'Yeah. He says only 7 died smoked. So what…?'

SAVE YOUR BACON?

'Forget recreational poisons Ann, life a sexually transmitted
disease. Yet allergies, arthritis, ageing have been alleviated
by changed diets. Cauliflower, broccoli, citrus fruits, nuts
and whole grains rich in antioxidants,
All fight free radicals.
That is, unstable oxygen molecules which can cause cancer.

Do pork eaters become chemically enhanced pigs?'

DECIDUOUS

Ignoring God, Caesar kissed our soil. Then Cromwell. As if
the same man, their feed faded as quickly as parchment.
Other conquerors followed…
When William the First of England took up the axe, the
Saxons hid in tress, When William Caxton took
up printing history…
…all the trees in Europe trembled.

WIND GOD

Dust everywhere. Red cheeks bulging, the cherub, like a balloon, was blowing up a planet. Then asthma, choking. Every cough, another galaxy appeared, his bad breath reaching every corner of every ailing cosmos. The cherub needed attention. So, in his own image, he created man. To clean up the chaos…?

OMENS…?

'Nothing lasts and nothing's new, Ann.
Egypt, Greece, Rome, Great Britain, all declined as Empires,
Their civilizations all collapsing.

When rulers
Gold palaces,
Poverty increases.

Power to the petrified…? Sand, rock, marble, bones,
Cobblestones, clay, all crumble.
Spring crocus still appear through
Concrete…!

DROUGHT?

'FIND WATER!' ordered the Chief
But his son found a desert Songbird.
So the Chief sent his daughter as well
Both children danced in the rain, the bird sweetly singing…
Dying of thirst and to stop children dancing
The Chief caged the songbird.
It stopped singing
It stopped raining

ON THE EDGE

Above city cries, an Alien cries. Raw drugs claw his guts.
Blind pin sears his brain-cells…agonies too inner to yell
aloud

Only beguiling death…falling…
…From that skyscraper windowsill can cure…
…Bystanders, with staccato breaths, baying for blood…
Crazed with vertigo, the copper yells.
'Don't f…fall or I'll shoot…!'

SCORPIO?

Lemon the lemming couldn't jump. Why should she die
young?
As the last lemming dived over the scorpion, clifftop Scamp
Appeared saying, 'Jump for joy!'
Full of tenderness, Scamp gave Lemon a hug, stinging her
With his tail. 'Change or die,' whispered Scamp.
Falling in love…
Lemon drowned…Laughing…!

ALIVE ALIVE O!

To leader pack of obedient dogs. Devoted to young mum
Trees frogs. Starling murmur, wren's moss nest firmer.
Many hidden lives in logs.

No nice way of killing life whether by poison or knife.
Tell corpse fly to its face I'll create and replace
All pests to reduce world strife…?

HONEYPOT

Two bees in a jam-jar heaving with honey plus two
Large ice-cubes. Over-feeding bees kept farting, ice
Melting floods, Bees crying, "We're unprotected!"
Too fat to fly, the bees stung each other, both dying in
Their last golden smear.'

'Grandad, wasps survive stinging,'
Protested Ann.
'Wasps don't make honey, darling

FACING DEATH

In Garth Castle's icy cellar dungeon a blind Mask-maker
Moulded his last mask – his own. This monster mask,
Like others before, he tried on.
Shrieks!
It won't peel off. Faceless corpses rise from coffins.
All scream for their faces, their own last lost death-masks.
They grab one. The mask-maker's skull.

GOBBLE-GOBBLE

'How many stockings filled like bad teeth...felled firs
Decorated like war veterans...non-organic baubles...
Obese birds plucked stuffed with wine drenched guts…'

'Who said Father Christmas came from inside hollow earth?
Men from monkeys...or turkeys from dinosaurs, Grandad?
On telly, arson, burglaries, terrorists populating heaven.
How awful…'
BELCH!

WORMS - 1 -

Worms dream of holes beyond mouths of moles and their
fat girth; Seeking ends to their low life, far removed from
landlocked earth
Uplifted by songbird's springtime wife
In high-flown nest screeching chicks
Needing another fix
There, dreaming of Black Holes
Dead just finding a high-flown flight furthering life's
might….?

WORMS - 2 -

Buried under stark smelly carparks how many dead worms
and silent larks worms with earthquakes will return
Likely then to discern
Between organic farmers and property sharks.
On the whole inside each hole, burrowing moles
Full of worms though they'd rather fly inside a bird
As if promotion not absurd.

WORLD SNAIL - 1 -

On windy world watch small Snail
Unfurled off the potter's wheel
Future feeling real his home a safe spiralled dome
Yet so easy to crush its lunch for mistle thrush
Relying on your glue showing no fear
Of fearing sparkling path of smear
A predator's clue that maybe death's overdue

WORLD SNAIL - 2 -

Despite your fear, tired bloodshot world,
Like our Snail in thickest rain, undulating, suppurating,
You live not in vain.

In searing deadly draught if fearing time runs out,
Your shell is firm so do not fret or squirm and don't forget,
Oh, Windy World Snail, we all leave a trail.

WORD SNAIL - 3 -

While world cliff-hangers are collapsing fast
Flooded homes on lands that won't last
On the White Cliffs of Dover and as you lean over
Ignore the dangers below, suicides won't enhance life's flow.
For survival's not by chance
Even in France.

Oh, windy World Snail
Loving
Life
Can never fail.

PAGAN PILGRIMAGES?

'Why not chat with pine or graveyard yew…?'
'Ann best chose a silver birch
'Nature's our church. Not praying on oaken pew,'
'What's wrong Grandad, me crying out,
"No more, dear sycamore, you litter lout"'?
'I do agree, plane to see as any tree
My Annie Green's not evergreen insane!'

SOUL BUDDIES

'Old Grandad, feels nice getting old,
Your blood running cold,
On ice no longer bold.'
'Young Ann, feels nice you taking hold, not being cajoled
Filtering what you're told,
Removed from family fold on my advice.
Needs no bells ringing
Our spirits singing'
'My best friend our love won't end.'

GETTING YOUNG

A bud is not a dud
Because not yet in full flower.

And lead is not yet dead
Believing in gold its full power.
With guided clear aims no past sighted foe maims
So, when in shock
Try not to scold the ticking clock
The first time we feel old.

GETTING YOUNGER

'A bloom is not in gloom when enjoying each sunlit hour.
Treasured bright gold will not dim when we feel too sour.
And Soul dearest Ann like a glass bowl can
Provide whatever we choose.'
'So, age for the ancient Sage
Is deciding to dance in the brightest golden shoes.'

CONVERSATION

'Don't look, Ann. Yes, you like to laugh…'
'Grandad, I'm imaging tigers in a bath,
Trying to wash behind their ears - OH!'
'Warned you. 18-years-old meat meal,
2,000 pounds of rare animal shot for Twitter,
black African giraffe shot
By a white American, rifle-toting tourists, courtesy
of South Africa.

SALAD DAYS

'Darling, eating out why me gets a dead slug…? YUK!
In my lettuce - a frog - ALIVE!'
'Improvement! Transformation, rebirth,
The circulation of colourful life-forms.
4,800 frogs from…'
'Darling, shut up my prince, why never you?'
On entering, 'Send love to the chef.'
'Cooked lettuce?'

'Tasty legs, Oh Madame mine!'

RICH SPECIES

In rain forests newly found, the rain frog with defences profound
Against enemy snake…… Sneaking close…Seems too gross.
By inflating its squeaking form…
…into a massive size…by this trick
No-one needlessly dies. To environment adapted,
Not when captured.
New creatures discovered
Every year…While known wildlife species…
…disappear.

ANN GREEN

Fourteen-year-old Ann forgiving Earth
Death with no brief for re-birth
As if Spring is not real or rains on no wheel
Each ship's cabin a sad short-term berth.

Our Ann Green as an early Indigo Lass
In Welfareland leading the mass
Blocks authorities, blooms priorities
Sharing left brain head-talk stale gas?

FROGGIE'S FROGHORN

FROGGIE'S FROGHORN - 1 -

Ann taught Grandad how to act
A talent he had so far lacked.
Ready to perform, survival the norm
Their 'laughing' audience was fully packed

SITTING ON HIS BROWN LOTUS LEAF
BOTH FROGGIE'S EYES FILLED UP WITH GRIEF
WITH WEEPING FROGGIE - *Mock weeping*
THE POND SALT SOGGY
POISONED ALL GOLDFISH UNDERNEATH

ON GOLDFISH SANDBANK SAT GOLLY - *Jolly laughing*
ON FISH-OIL FAT, RICH WITH BROLLY,
HE SAID, "I'M GOD NOW!
"I'LL SHOW RAIN CLOUDS HOW
TO MAKE YOU SALT POND MORE JOLLY." - *Lots of laughter*

BUT FROGGIE SOON SNORING OUT LOUD - *Snoring*
FELL ASLEEP IN A BLACK DREAM CLOUD
TILL HIS INNER VOICE
MADE HIM REJOICE
SAYING, "PRINCE, YOU'LL SOON BE SO PROUD!" - *All repeat*

ON SEEING POOR FROGGIE SO GLAD
THAT FAT GOLDFISH GOLLY GOT MAD - *Mock angry growl*
"EXPLAIN TO ME FROG
"HOW IN THIS SALT BOG
"YOU'RE DAMN HAPPY," HE SAID, "NOT SAD." - *Happy clappy*

"I SEE MIRACLES MADE OF LOVE,"
REPLIED FROGGIE, "FROM ABOVE. - *Point upwards*

"SO ALL LIKE CAN LIVE
"I ASK MAY I GIVE -
"BE WITH GOD, GOLDFISH, HAND-IN-GLOVE." –
hands interweave

BEFORE GOLLY COULD GULP OR GLARE
A DANDELION SEEN IN THE AIR
DANCED UP FROGGIE'S NOSE
AND TICKLED HIS TOES - *Giggles*
HE AIMING SNEEZES EVERYWHERE. - *Multi sneezes*

ALL ROUND FROG'S NOW DRY FISHLESS POND
LITTLE SEEDLINGS FIRST TO RESPOND
SOON SHOT UP GREEN SHOOTS - *uncurl 8 fingers*
AS TADPOLES
AND NEWTS
JOINED FLOWERS ALL RED, BLUE AND BLONDE.

"YOU MUST BE GOD, FROGGIE. "THEY CRIED,
- *Repeat*
"TO MAKE WATER WET, TURN THE TIDE!" – *Repeat*
BUT SUDDENLY STOPPED
HIS SNEEZES GOT BLOCKED - *All pinch nose*
BEFORE FROGGIE'S GOOD NEWS SPREAD WIDE.

FOR CREATURES DYING OUT ON DRY SAND
WITH SALT TEARS THEY MADE NO GREEN LAND
TILL SHOT TO THEIR KNEES
BY FROGGIE'S BEST SNEEZE - *LOUDEST SNEEZE EVER*
ALL MET AT THE POND AS IF PLANNED.

FROM FRESH POND THEY ALL DRANK THEIR FILL
- *GULPS*
PRAISING FROGGIE THEIR LATEST THRILL:
LIONS AND LAMBS DANCING - *WITH HANDS*?
SNEEZES ENHANCING – *SNEEZING FIT*
THE LOVE BETWEEN BOTH JACK AND GILL - *All hugs*!

QUICKER THAN FILLED UP WITH GEYSERS
THE PONG OVERFLOWS WITH SNEEZES - ***multiple sneezes***
"WE LOVE YOUR PRINCE FROG!" - ***Repeat phrase***
SINGS EACH CAT AND DOG
DRINKING NOW AS MUCH AS EACH PLEASES.

SNORING LOUD ON HIGH LOTUS LEAF
GOLDFISH THANKS FROGGIE FROM BENEATH
AND ALL POND LIFE TOO
SHINES LIKE MORNING DEW
SURVIVAL THE WORLDWIDE BELIEF. –

BELIEF!

BELIEF

BELIEF!

FOR SAFE KEEPING?

Power potential castle's Keep. BBC serves folks still asleep
Sunday for wildlife and religious strife
RE and survival for plebs too deep? 'Ann, try to hold the
same fistful of river water in your right hand - and twice.
Or capture the cold draft from my study door in a vice?'

BIOBANKING?

All cooked veg once were weeds,
Profits or patents aiming to colonise seeds
As the extraordinary succeeds. When LSD Leads global
economy –
Cows', chickens', swine's, mankind's
Diseases,
No matter how high hedge funds.

As if bodies in ice, will cryonics suffice
Better than a natural forest fire
For resurrecting life?

DECISIONS?

Decarbonisation decide so not more global warming
deride.
Hot air overheats, Profits' pundit cheats
If Earth not loved, where do we hide?
Will electric plugs for driverless cars
Cause more solar panels on new rooves
As if windmills Dutch landscape mars. How soon
Before each of us scared moves…
To……Where…?

FOOD BANKS?

Buying *plastic* tubes for human resuscitation, non-biodegradable for global digestion? This is a paradox based on binary coding.
At least the path less travelled is centre of roads.

Roadkill fills no raptors' crops. Farmers' crops fill the crow as old cronies grumble.
'Like you, grandad. After every grumble, you tumble…!'

SEAWEEDS?

35% of fish thrown back into the sea as unsellable.
Certain stocks dangerously diminished

'Superfoods powerful disease-blockers, aiding longevity grandad
And could be your lifesaver!'

'Ann dear, to live the life given me is braver.
Nutrition's future is found in the ocean, said Jacques Cousteau.'

'Who? Some film star, was Jack?'

GAME AND SET?

Big Game hunters bristling with muscles, bullets, suntan lotion, plus bottled insect repellents with flasks of more than water.

Big beasts beware.
Heads on drawing-room walls with decapitated foxes as domestic trophies and the horns of regal stags.

Holy statues made of stone or porcelain
Have been known to weep.

SENTRY ISLAND

Before Canadians were invented and civilised the Bay area
they called Hudson, polar bears were roaming sentries.
Now popular for anglers fishing for food.
On a visit with his family, Aaron protected his schoolgirl
daughter from a hungry polar bear having found no full
trashcans
Bear shot.

FAMILY PRIDE

With sharpened axes, wire-cutters, powerful rifles with
silencers, food for three days a poacher gang stalking all
rhino horns
In a Game Reserve.
Lions, watchful guardians…LEAPT!

Reserve owner, Mr Fox, found six shoes
And three severed heads with Afros, unidentified. Unlike
the tourists next day also baying for blood.

STOCKINGS

Wild zebras are protected by their stripes from starving
predators. Dysphasia disorientates big beasts as they charge,
the weaving would-be four-legged meals running for their
lives.

Horseflies bite retired donkeys even in Sanctuaries.

One such was protected, not with insect repellent but with
Black and white striped socks
Then unbitten.

SUGAR BUZZ

One-part water, two parts water in a vet's syringe.
A novel medicine for a weary insect - 'where the bee sucks' –
In order to regain enough energy to fly away.

One more pollinating human food.

Meanwhile, bee numbers are being decimated by
Use of pesticides
And loss of habitat.

HOT FUZZ

Countryside police have it cushy?
What with sheep rustling not knife gangs?
Rescuing injured cyclists from muddy ditches
And swans poisoned by lead fishing-gear.

One such constabulary let fly a feisty swan from a squad car
Much to their amusement as if replicating
A scene from a comic movie.

WRETCHED GULLS?

Thirsty being in soaring temperatures with water shortages
And seawater not desalinized. Time for some cool beer.
And for scavengers.

Falling from a roof dead drunk, or reeling about on beaches,
Boozed up seagulls have been rescued by vets
Employed by the RSPCA.
One threw up -
On its kindly Keeper.

THREESOMES?

Which birds now as rare as rural busses?
Too many minus signs too few pluses
Matters conservation in Nature's Reservation so far protected,
By the public at large neglected.
Breeding pairs with only one chick thriving,
Even human sperm counts diving. '
Prayers Ann won't help dying cuckoo-clocks lay fertile eggs,'

SEVEN HUES?

Scores of songbirds on staves of branches.
A woodlark with tonsillitis had admired kingfishers.
Inspired by forest choristers the artist dozing
She selected flakes of glinting paint from portraits of
Goldfinches, siskins, bullfinches, woodpeckers.

With sprinkled coloured flakes over her dull feathers, in
song.
She thanked the resident rainbow.

GOOD GROWTH

Seedlings treated like classroom schoolkids…?
To Box One the scientist keeps repeating. "You're beautiful,
Healthy, good!"
To Box Two, 'You're ugly, stunted, No good!' To the third
box they leave them to nature. The first lot grows up tall.
The second lots small, the third normal.

Pants have green ears?

TIMETABLED

36 multi-coloured youngsters being force-fed; every 40
minutes, bells helping headaches, another waiter delivered
assorted foods

Monday, like Friday, was hamburgers; junket, pizza, rats,
doughnuts, frogs' legs and candy floss.
Captives allergic to e-additives had no option but to swallow
hard. Anxious slaves got the trots – back home. From
whence? WHY?

CASE HISTORY

Engrossed in the unhappy moment unable to concentrate
on History. Sucks pencil-point.
In Maths, she obsessively collates young suicide figures.
In geography – all roads lead…to death.
Hordes Italian wines, not French, despite her dad
absconding
to Paris. Claims in ancient Rome she died of
lead-poisoning.

Should Ann Green get expelled…?

CHOSEN LIVES?

'Pollution, doctors employed despite miners
And steelworkers redundant.
With more enforced leisure, State should pay nominal
allowances to citizens, excluding robot slaves.
695,000 UK folks on the autistic spectrum.
'1 in 4 gay Ann, and same percentage get cancer.
Self-rejection, like resentment, lethal.
Mothers' milk radio-active,
Their nipples barely weeping

ENTERPRISE

GRANDAD - £100 down payment…!
HEADTEACHER - Ann's new school investment.
Refundable anti-litter fund. Deposit gains interest. Earnings
from recycled tins, paper, clothes, all swelling the fund.
'However, if Ann drops litter, vandalises…fine! Convicted,
£1 per item. Deduced from your down-payment.'
'GRANDAD - All accountable. Good!'

Church mouse

As Mouse and Moggy rang church bells, no-one appeared.
Starving, snowbound, Moggy meditated as Mouse slid down
the bell-rope. Their paws in high-five, cat and mouse prayed
for miracle food till, Moggy pronounced, "God helps those
who help themselves…!" Poor church mouse grabbed a
mouthful
of cat's rump and scarpered…!

FATAL FOREPLAY

Chain-smoking, millionaire Mick lowered into his bathwater
An electric fire. Power-cut!
Mick jumped off his yacht…cradled by pearl-divers.
Stroking gold coffin, Mick leapt from his penthouse…onto
Window-cleaners' platform!
Sobbing, he sucked his bruised thumb. Prognosis - cancer.
Now refusing suicide,
He decided to live a better life.
Make a bigger, fatter fortune!

SOLE SURVIOR

Angling for Sharkface, eyebrows writhed like frying
caterpillars…
Sweaty eyeballs bulging…Ted pulling fishing-rod…then...
SPLASH!
Fishing-tackle drowned; seawaves eerily calmed when
suddenly –
BITE!
Sharkface loomed up through oil-slick blanketed with
human hair.
In his grin a boot. In that a foot. Sharkface from below,
jawbones…pulling…pulling Ted…
SPLASH!

FROZEN FUTURES

God of Robots, protect our sperm-banks
Whales…dolphins…dodos, preserve all species
Their seeds frozen in test-tubes.

Unite against cosmic catalytic enemies…
Nuclear slips…war…droughts…floods…famine…
Unto the revelations of fire and ice-flows.
Should humanity be included in this list, Lord?
Saints preserve us!
Longer to ponder, please…

RE-VOLUTIONS…?

Slavery	- Freedom	V	Chains…………?
English	- Free Speech	V	Dictatorships…..?
French	- Privilege, Peasants	V	Aristocracy……...?
American	- Democratic Dream	V	Gun Kaw………..?
Nuclear	- Energy, Power	V	Peace…………..?
Information	- Webs	V	Brain drains……..?
Space	- Interstellar colonisations	V	Invasions……….?
Spiritual	- Dogma, Priestcraft	V	DIY DIVINITY…?

'Why must history repeat itself, Ann…?'

DOLPHINS' BALLET

As with Hawaii fewer days of annual rain, worldwide
weather trend becoming so plain.

Sleeping on beaches near dolphins a treat,
Wet through all night with no retreat
Then swim with dolphins in a foul mood
Keeping their distance, they won't intrude!

Me happy next day, gladly the dolphins play!

SAPPING BLOOD

Ages of blood sacrifices past
Now symbolised in Christians' communion rituals?
Believing all came from the same god, slit stomachs gaping
From throat to navel.
Heavy crops the expected reward as with Spanish goats
Hurled from tall towers, bulls slaughtered in public
As sophisticated as Romans watching lions killing
Christians…?

SAFE JAWS?

Human fatalities greater in war-torn lands
Or on pirate-infested oceans?
During World War 2, now mostly dangerous to bathers.
Are blue sharks attacking in packs?
Beware hammerheads, polluted bull sharks and property
sharks
Giving others bad reputations. Yet since 1900, only 50
people
Have died from shark attacks.

SIGHTINGS?

Off the Spanish Mediterranean Coast. a wildlife conservation crew
Spotted a great white shark;
Filmmakers not after rumours but evidential footage.

This shark species plus shortfin mako, porbeagle numbers declining.
70m per year killed for their fins.
More dangerous than top marine predator, drivers, fast food,
Plastic pollution, climate change.

NATIONAL MEADOWS DAY

Varieties of bugs, bees, butterflies, mammals, birds and wildflowers
On modern farmlands – unlikely?
Since the 1930s, 97% species-rich grasslands, gone.
Bring back widely early purple orchid, mountain pansy, cowslips
Rock roses and bilberries.
Thanks to the charity the National Trust
Hundreds of acres of flower-rich Derbyshire farmlands
Have been bought.

FULL MOON MEDITATION - 1 -

The Arcane School celebrates three yearly festivals.
At Eastertime there's an Aries full moon gathering.
Time for again reawakening,
Representing resurrection
Of dormant matter rising
As with the human spirit.
Personal leadership with a forward-forging energy
Reminds us all life is seasonal, circular
And rebirth applies to all on earth

FULL MOON MEDITATION - 2 -

Wesak celebrates the exact time of the Taurus full moon
When the Buddha some say appears
In a Himalayan valley to disciples.
His blessings being so powerful
Most need to retreat taking uplifts of energy
In alignment with the keynote of Taurus
To live more consciously
Within their
Soul Cluster.

FULL MOON MEDITATION - 3 -

The law the lesser follows the greater is indicated,
The Gemini full moon yearly inviting humanity to unify
And synthesise the two selves, higher and lower.
Ancient wisdom always invited at-one-ment in divine harmony
With the music of the spheres, to and beyond ...
Back to before the big...
BANG!

ALKALISE OR DIE?

Overly acid rain should be neutralised.
Alkalinity in water effects all vegetation.
In Australia they've increased crop yield, accelerated green germination, cleaned lakes and ponds, reduced biological stress
From microwave radiation, and increased good negative ions
Using orgone technology.
DNA is debilitating nutritional value from non-foods
By radiation and toxins

ABATTOIRS

Cuddle piglets, kitten and puppy-dog. Then cook them and
savour with expensive delicacy, leg of a frog. Orphaned
six=year-old Ann heard Bleeding piglets squeal
For their mum.
Blades of grass don't feel because dumb?
Fertilised eggs faint…their friends in hot water.
Vegans claim veggie numbers soar once they've seen
slaughter.

EXTANCT?

As man unkindly and systematically eradicates life's variety
From our earth, its species maybe safest
At the bottom of oceans' wombs.
'Extinct' coelacanth, a fossil' for 66 million years
Was discovered in 193
.
Finder Marge had the corpse stuffed as are other rare
specimens in museums, frozen zoos like mausoleums.

HERETICS?

Bathers on rafts lie along streams
Aware not all is as it seems,
To youngsters endow Harry Potter's power
Let well-meaning bigots steam.
Dancing in Stonehenge with Druids,
Pagans fear Satan not Pan.
In Nature celebrate The Plan.
Stars stones trees,
All creatures with bees.
Sacred solstice rituals worship all these.

COLOR-BLIND?

Red Indians and cowboys of old
Black Red not White words some scold
Wild weeds different hues lack prejudicial views
No colour-bar blooms grow tall and bold.
Imagine a chameleon blushing in shame
When a palate of quick changes its game.
Paintings in many guises protected
As prey gets detected!

GUIDANCE?

Freewill facilitates many faiths, no matter in things or
wraiths
Some aim to rate ALL everywhere
As with Living Insignia in Delaware.
Local butterfly, grey fox, blue hen,
Slogan – Endless Discoveries – with own flag and Seal
But then Wikipedia shows no chapel or church
As societies towards the secular lurch?

NATURE MAGAZINE

Rapidly Indigos evolve, wisdom gained on Souls' revolve.
Recalled Atlantis deluge Rebels divulged cause solve?
Teachers - 'Each has a disorder.'
Woodlands kids' play experiences broader
Thousands holding rosebuds watched
6-year-old appear on Stage and wave.
Buds became beautiful roses.
Result, astonished, gasping, cynical mind closes –
Teachers grasping but not…?

SALT MARSHES

Same sky black and white clouds – magic. Coastal erosion
– tragic –
Black for droughts, white for sun.
Meteorologists share doubts though Met Office predict
2040's heatwaves. Salt marshes serve food webs supplying
nutrients.
Sea rising causes waterlogs killing tress, grasses, threatening
fish nurseries, marsh tit, heron, egret, ibis, wren –
Not sure when.

MOANING LAWNS

Love the scent of new-mown grass like outdoor morning
toast?
A sign of blades being in a state of chemical distress.
Released organic compounds help form new cells
Healing wounds faster, preventing bacterial infection
And fungal growth, like antibiotics.
Mowing humans oxygenate the atmosphere
Grazing animals with methane farts.

MOOING MUMS

Worms for healthy soil and garments in silk
No cystitis or healthy grass for winter milk
Coconuts soy and almond milk don't count
Factory farming Mother Nurture denied
Millions from disease died.
Hormone-treated beef genetically modified crops
Help environmentally friendly ecological cops
Mother Nature relishes every carcass.
Re-cycling never stops.

HORSEPLAY

Near stables with ponds, woodland areas grassy,
In hot weather horseflies bite not just the classy
Clegs's dark insect itchy sores
Can be worse with sharper claws.
Female horseflies' bloodsuckers before laying eggs
Can bite through clothes and bare legs, yet pollinating flowers
And providing foods' source for animals' powers.

FROM STAR DUST?

On earth's shrinking regulated room
In healthy times white shone seaside spume
And so is it still with plastic junk
Till plastic coffins make chimneys fume.
Non-organic due to Boffins Air-polluted coughs in the offing
The longer we breathe
Resultant to leave
Non-biodegradable coffins.

BACK AS STARDUST? - 1 -

Rewilding ruins archaeological sites,
Cyclic seasons like Passages of Rites,
Less hedges from woodland cuttings
Despite worried tuttings
Species diversity depletion reducing sights.
Now bees in cities more than in woods
As kindly conservation unfolds.
Some lambs born blind. Less blindness we find
In proud farmers with less profit inclined.

DISCOVERIES

'Aliens built Stonehenge, Ann? – Or maybe weren't.
Bones' shapes become crystalised when burnt
By Neolithic males from South West Wales,
This scientists latterly learnt.
Moya Caldecott's head against a Tall Stone
Captured karmic records etched. Insights overstretched?
Her Third Eye got a running documentary
Of Bronze Age battles not far-fetched.'

AS STARDUST? - 2 -

Suckling calves an accessory. In wildlife a necessity.
God's University gives life Diversity
Grazing cattle need no pessary!
Rewilding ruins archaeological sites;
Circular seasons more as climate backbites.
Landowners' woodland pledges provide cuttings for hedges.
Not walls. Neolithic Welshmen Stonehenge erected,
Crystallised bones resurrected. DNA dates them to the day?

BACK AS STARDUST? - 3 -

New forests for wholeness and renewal.
That's Old Mother Nature's healthy school.

Queen with us thank woodlands creatures' banks.
Wood-stoves' logs leave where insects can refuel.
Old folks put on ice to die or on mountains to rot.
Pacifist Egyptian vulture no Pharaoh's flesh got.
Cadavers? Earth-to-earth better for horticulture?

GRASSING

'Sit babes-in-arms on a green lawn,
Especially offspring city born.
Though bottom nappied, their reaction rapid.
Despite covered arse one look at the grass
They lift their legs all forlorn.
Ann don't wed a townie twerp, feeling fruit-picking
And farming too hard work.
Forest Schools for interconnections.
Forget countryside defections.'

AMBLES IN THE BRAMBLES?

'Ann, the colour green can work of parts of our psyche
which needs further development.

That's why, if feeling down, it's pleasing to the spirit to stroll
in emerald fields and fertile forests and feel carpeted green
under your feet while overhead,
Soothing canopies of leafy boughs, birds singing brightly.'

COUNTRY CRAFTS

Plastic curbed many crafts. The use of willow serves many
arts
Curing folks' headaches while fringing tranquil lakes.
Weaving baskets opens hearts. Engravings on birch wood
burnt
Another craft so rarely learnt.
Biodegradable wrapping has all life-lovers clapping,
Like paper round sweets, including sweetmeats.
Man's greed most natural reserves sapping.

VEGAN VILLAINS?

Necessary fare has a high price.
For pockets and endangered tress
Whether chickpeas or avocado pears
Threatened meat-eaters these to appease
Or illegal collectors of wild birds' eggs
Thieving criminal for 18 months jailed
Inside consuming scrambled eggs not frogs' legs
Chicken mums chick-breeding failed by merchants bird
lives assailed.

DARKNESS

If distant dates, dawns no daylight
If man bloats our frail planet with blight.
What might get recreated will get incinerated.
Mankind, reimagine ego's Might
Earth's kindergartens, some sun-soaked some Spartan
To higher classes past Paul Tarsus respond
Heaven on earth now disheartened
Nature Spirits in the slough of despond.

WINTER WOES

White brown black bread or muffins
Bird lovers would not feed to puffins
Scampi caviar or flying fish roe to Tower ravens
Tame rook or carrion crow feed bamboo to baboons
To swans that starve so stately and suave, feed mixed veggie
diet
not bread alone before they're only bone.

AIRY TALES?

Rare toad stolen - who'd nick one
When so tricky to lick one?

Their skin said to heal but not as a meal,
Easy now to pick the sick one!
No princess locked in police bangles
As the steel chain jangles.
If only she'd taken a different road
And kissed the healing toad!

ENDANGERED?

'School education politicalised
Student's true Soul not Self-realised
Find out who you are Ann, all your potential scan
For the State don't get standardised.
Cloning a waste of resources
No aiding inner discourses
Discerning your dreams, you blood as clean streams
Only those afraid join forces.
Precaution worries. Prevention hurries?'

STERILISED CITIES?

Less pesticides biodegradable bags manicured grasslands
Starlings' swivel eyes long legs feathers flashed
Flocks roosting in trees dustbins bashed
They disabled Big Ben.
Some citizens rear 1 of 23 species of bees
As Rome's invaders in wet weather freeze.
No nectar as feed refusing to breed
Darwin's adaptation perceived need.

DISABLED LINKS

Flower powers' hippy sixties celebrated all from plants to
pixies
Earth's bio-feedback self-regulating
Love's Creations forever gestating.
Mankind denying his faults, James Lovelock insight assaults
Comic life interconnected, deaths making no distinction
Never dejected by extinction.
As burger bars fell jungle trees
Man-friendly healing plants not now found in these

DISLOCATIONS

Silent Spring DDT blitzkrieg garden birds dead
Rachel Carson's warning still shouts
Victims quickened on death's roundabouts.
27,000 species out-for-the-count
More room less health as pollutants mount.
TNT obliterating DDT ecologists' not deterred
Unlike the lovesongs of each silent bird.
Seashells on hilltops till timewaves' reprise

Oceanic floods refreshing these.

SHREWD

'Tree shrews used to climbers challenging mountain
reaches
As they wade through jungle tangles avoiding giant leeches;
From Elementals into minerals, next into plants,
Then monkey shrews sire these till apes as in chimpanzee.
Ann, don't fairy tales tell us more about existence as with
fables
- So-called fantasy - enables further
Transcendence?'

MAN'S ESTATE

Classy landowners' aristocratic privatisation
Once patronising peasants' deprivation
Squires' estates how vast now as in the past
Unlike Longleat's acres providing creatures' safe vocation
Predators and vicious vexation.
A lordly haven on earth. Spend much more than your
pennyworth. Grounds Capability Brown landscaped
Rare beasts from extinction escaped.

RELILIANCE

Return to our roots helped by local Self-reliance?
Encourage resource conservation
Within a wider compliance?
A 50/50 chance of keeping earthlings
A 2-degree level of warming incompatible
With exponential economic growth,
No matter how the capitalists are loath
To claim they're to blame.

Top-down unelected autocracy the enemy of democracy?

MORE RELILIANCE

No castles built by beasts fearing death
Though weapons used so their offspring can share breath.

Insects' wield chemical warfare before the nestlings' welfare,
Cubs and chicks trained to survive within their environment
With no harmful artificial implement causing slanderous waste.
Faeces fuel further growth. Even with slow tree-hugging sloth.

SLY

After watching, sniffing, listening, foxes snoop
Causing slaughter in chicken coop
On wilful killing spree with wildest beastly glee
Blood lust ready to vandalise unguarded henhouses by surprise.
Gearing up Redcoats' speeding tally-ho's spree
No empathy spared, some wildlife snared,
Net banquet for laird, poachers unprepared their deeds well dared!

FLY

Fly-tipper with plastic insects to catch fish on boats
With punishing lead-floats stuck in swan's throats…?
Construction, landscape contractors, scrapyard operators
Motor and tire-repair shops
All dump so no health risk stops
Preventing hazardous material secrets like endless nuclear
waste
Dangerously legal – If not lethal?

Not so the dung beetle.

PROMISES PROMISES

Factory farming and domestic animal abuse
When does protesting become no use?
Tireless impassioned campaigner's pro-active complainers
With bottle deposit schemes versus climate change feigners.

Winning words we might vote for in hope.
When disillusioned best not to mope,
But get out there and contribute, forgetting those who love
refutes.

DIE

Mother cow no milk for her dead calf
Lambs for liver their lives not yet half
Netted skylarks writhe. What next won't survive?
Where plant Planet Earth's Cenotaph?
Schoolchildren in a slaughterhouse after farming
Maybe carnivore numbers harming,
Vegans more charming
Vegetarians and teetotallers less disarming,
More arms' manufacture alarming?

DROUGHTS

Sun's cycles and spots cause radiation.
Fewer means magnetic core dilation
Yellow sun now white. See that as all right
South hemisphere beware conflagration.
Though for OK we employ the word cool Just 30-degree students
Still in school
Too hot to study, even in the nuddly, in some hot States
Skin-dipping the rule.

FLOODS

Elements revenge on man
Worshippers rate Satan not Pan
St. Peter warned, '*The fire next time.*'
Warnings from Noah should also chime.
Climate migrants with thousands still displaced.
Multiple floods in the Americas
Through Causes not faced.
Glacial seas and lakes melt faster.
Seas and rivers rise drowning world disaster?

FIRES

Fires from near Artic Circle to Sweden Portugal Greece
Saddleworth Moor's carbon-rich shouldering peat
Didn't cease cooking worms, golden plovers, voles and insects
No longer. Feeding amphibians mammals birds snakes rare mountain hares, Brush burning for extensive miles
Nasa' Tera Satellite records what's likely to ignite
Mother Nature's indefectible might.

EMISSIONS

Lightning strikes helped early fire-shaping of many landscapes.
Woodash good for providing micronutrients for man and apes Potassium phosphorous magnesium leads
To fertilisation of seeds.' Healthy new growth
Traditionally in agriculture fire used. Sometimes legally
As with charcoal barbecues with wood chips.
Illegal bonfires and biomass burn in toxic rubbish-tips.

ITCHING

Cacti thrive in heated kitchens. Heat suits fleas,
Dogs left in car ovens windows locked.
One sweating Iranian householder couldn't enter his house
For battalions of fleas. Attacking his naked legs
Natterjack toads leave their water nurseries
Before they're fully developed.
Gardeners, fill up ponds before hosepipe-ban.
For house sparrows need water.

FLASH POWER

Rarely known to lose her rag,
Her work ethic will never lag.
Legging it through hills letting go earth's ills
The bombs' button in her handbag.
Before skeleton trees blackened, blasted local hills flattened,
Green fields in flames with flowers Man's greed
For conquering new ground, his godly power's slackened.

SEEKERS

Beavers like all wildlife is never unemployed
Though food scarcity can make them so annoyed.
Fighting to eat, fighting to breed. Even in zoos with daily feed
See passionate pioneers as animal behaviour researchers,
Endless the probing human quest

Scientists studying leeches or lurches
Since curiosity will never know rest.

LAST STRAW

'Ann save all countries in Esperanto
Especially polluting traders in China and USA
'Grandad, I can teach babies to drink without plastic straws
Without sugary dinks. Better for reusable teeth
Not that clever but I don't like wars.'
Ann then reads, 'Toothpaste contains chemicals
Artificial sweeteners
And fluoride poisoning bloodstreams.'

SHAPNEL?

'Priest, 1.1/2 thousand pounds? I'll re-pay…'
'Ann, money mustn't make money. Only work…'
'Must be a way round all laws
Can I borrow, say 1.1/2? You make a profit?'
'1.1/2 years ago interest illegal.
Today, I say, Earn pocket-money, Ann.'
'No profit?'
'Prophet? I'm a modern Mullah so yes, profit.'

LITTLE FAITH?

'Got us believing in fairies, Father Christmas, then say
"Fake news!" 'Dad, you screamed IMAGINATION! Me
seeing UFOs…laughed when I cried. That ghost spoke my
name.
Off to see Grandad…'
'Invisible inventions!'
'All inventions started off invisible.
Dad, you taught me to tell lies. 'Cos you won't hear my
truth.'

ALRIGHT JACK?

'My Right to hit you, son.'
'I'll kick your dog, dad!'
'BITE!'
'Bitch bit me. RABIES…!'
'Treatment's free.'
'Drive me!'
'Human Rights. Here on radio…
'I'm bleeding, dad…
Into phone, listening: 'Yes, freedom from fear, hunger, disease,
All International Rights. Next caller, please!'
'Listeners, dad's killing me.' 'Jack, you're homeless!'

ASH CASH

'If 8 out of 10 shopkeepers sell me fags and illegal sales
make millions each year Grandad, shouldn't tobacco
companies sponsor cancer research, not sport…?'
'Apprentice Ann, in soccer the World Cup's your golden goal,
so why smoke? To be one of the lads?' 'Yeah. But not like dad, right.'

CAPITALS?

'Knife Crime…300 languages in my school. Outside, homeless beggars common as crack. What they learn at school useful for NOW? Or me, Grandad. Home school me, eh? I've checked. It's legal. No expensive Uni. Give money to Shelter.'
'Inexpensive, good ideas. Spare – enough for one, Ann?'

'Spare enough for ALL!"

PECKING ORDERS?

Dominance?
Conquer territory, food supplies, shelter requirements, peers,
Mating preferences and safety from predators.
Inbuilt weapons in DNA. Yet how do female wild tigers, mostly solitary, 'Know' to grow white patches behind their ears?
These show cubs all is well, but disappear as ears flatten,
Warning cubs behind mum. Crouch.

ACCIDENTAL DEATH?

'Forty fags,' 'coughed up mum. Dad drunk said, 'Killing her, them fags!' Pinching cash from her bag, he lurches into the Off License.
Drinking outside, mate offered dad stolen fags and booze.
Threatened by yobs, dad staggered across the road…
Squeals of breaks - Screams.
'Safe with me, Ann.'
'Thanks, Grandad.'

'ENTERPRICES'?

GRANDAD:	– £100?
HEADTEACHER:	– Investment. Ann's future. Half to anti-litter-fund.
GRANDAD:	– Deposits gain interest…like antiques?
HEADTEACHER:	– Earnings from recycled tins, paper, Rubbish, uniforms swell funds. If Ann drops litter, vandalizes…
GRANDAD:	– Ann hates schooling…
HEADTEACHER:	– Good". £1 per item now cut from down-payments.
GRANDAD:	– All accountable. Good.

GRAN

Wrapped in a holy blue shawl she patiently waits
Water on the brain…the knees, incontinent at both icy
ends…
Surgery scars are savage wounds, body-hair exhausted
Grey bones brittle as sandstone breathing in rasping gasps
These death-rattles of Mother Earth…
Suggesting…that those who die…
Must diagnose their dust TOO LATE…?

PERFECT MURDER

In the acid bath she sits soused in toxic excrement,
Her chopped-up body savagely mutilated, ravished recklessly
Bereft of all warm comforting creatures
Each silent spring she chokes on aching screams…
Only 95% of Planet Earth remains arable
It's not just drought to blame…but man's slow erosion of proactive HOPES.

GREENER FAIRER?

'Hoped CFCs some football Club to join.'
Ann pulled down her skeleton mask, joined the break-in
That night they unplugged 22 polluting freezers
Like world clean Iceland.
Bejam good riddance!
Welcome ozone-friendly products.
A hole appeared in their plan to raise
Supermarket awareness – again. Ann's Police Uncle appeared
– Fair cop…?

NOT BOOKBOUND

My main fans don't buy my books Seems only their Third Eye looks
One smells the covers psychic the others.
Blind folk love bubbling brooks draped with willows
Fairies dancing on soft mossy pillows
Tender runners stirred by currents
Regal swans sedately cruising
Ducklings scuttling after mum, No life dumb.

REDUNANT?

'Ann, bodies don't need detoxing any more than you need boxing.
Internal organs act like sewers, kidneys, liver health renewers,
Radiance spirit restoring…?
Let all blood flow like a clean river Jesus' hands cured the lame
Might Gaia not do the same?
All life reaches higher
Never ceasing to aspire.

TIGER TIGER

Millionaire jails suspected killer
Later data heightened this murder thriller.
Released jungle female limped on wounded paw
Successfully cured behind cages
Mum produces 3 cubs more
Sumatran villagers' fears again soar
Till conservationist assuages anxieties
They persuade future societies like theirs
Co-habitation is Love's Way
Since raw Nature always shares?

SANE BELFREYS

Horseshoe bats noses squeaking
Night highways served by hedgerows speaking
Like all objects mapped by reverberating sound.
Law-protected Preservation orders slow worldwide peaking
Concern ringing alarm-bells all round
Cowpats bats feeding dung beetles breeding grubs
With hero Chris Packham set up Wildlife Clubs
Less pesticides, farming caring
Healthy environments sharing?

LESS BUMBLING

Grasslands preserved by weed hidden litter hairy
bumblebee's nest where they jitter, great tits, crows, mice
shelters invading.

Others heavy with honey as garden flowers parading and
hay meadows with wild clover, its scent spread through the
whole hive so more can survive, pollinating for us all health
help, heaven-sent.

DEATH-DEFYING

Kangaroo-legged hares; 360° vision; flattened in earth form,
Till coursing's starving dogs swarm.
Fleeing meadows alive. Safe in a cemetery thrive.

Farmers' barn owls hunt foraging fieldmice in grass
tussocks
Silent wings swooping in a trice
Yearly diet, 100,000 moles, heart-shaped face deceptive
No mercy shown, sloppy human sentimentality overblown?

PLEDGES PLUS

Mixed farming mixed grasses aiding birds like hedges
Harbouring chicks till each fledges
Meadow blooms garlanding rapefield edges
Slopes for snowfalls' kiddies' sledges
Beefeaters consuming more fruits and veges
Mad car disease prevAILS.
Pigeon Fanciers peregrine falcons on city ledges.
Drowning vans, no drains
Flash flood dredges
Despite politician's green pledges?

S. ISLAND NZ - 1 -

Darwin upended, Galapagos appended, unique sub-arctic
sea lions, like penguins, shelter in forest thicket,
Kiwis spying invertebrate, pick it.
Hot/cold clashing air causes deluges nurturing mosses'/
ferns' maturation. Bright parrots' damaging beaks
Burrowed chicks weasel seeks,
Glow-worm galaxies like spiders glued water-dribbles
Invite night insects for midnight nibbles.

S. ISLAND NZ - 2 -

Alps rising 7 meters daily snow-cover pieced by edelweiss
And artic buttercups as on long succulent earthworms
Giant snail sups massive mountain glaciers
Carelessly cascade crashing into cocktails of fresh and
saltwaters allowing calm coastal lagoons as mud-impeded
penguins' bathroom. Feathers re-oiled, battling battering
billows, violent surges catapult chicks for six.

CUTTINGS?

Old pond – frog jumps in – waters sound.
Lamp lit – moth no sin – killing ground
Clock hides nest – waif no house – cuckoo time
Mud glue - mind the ape – thinking cages
Bleached antler dismissed – stepping-stones - milestones
Plants hear riddles – saplings dissolve old bones
Disconnect God's phone – no koan a clone.

ORINENTEERING

Discovering psychic satnav, digging communal lav, bonfire
shooting sparks, sizzling sausages spit, dreams of lullaby
larks, woken by screeching owls seeking truffles hands
flexible trowels, ablutions in cold stream, groins flicked
with towels, naked in sweat lodges, storytelling on sheepskin
rugs, man-handled loaves in wodges, ember-cooked spuds
Scouts saluting hugs.

SNAKE OILS?

Rites of passage in nature's wilderness. Removal from family
home, meditating as rovers roam, feeling more powerful
and free, no further need for LSD, wise primitive bi-polar
bear liberty.
Earlier karma lamented, mental stability dented with
Aztec's morning glory or gohoba, like sleeping with cobra.

Welcome separation initiation
And return.

SYMBIOSIS

Micro/macrocosm innate in Soul's Creation
All life's seeds in slow Gestation
Sensing harmony needs balance, in all forms interlinked,
Despites minks that escape from fur farm, causing many
creatures harm, Indigenous creations awry, all on gerbil's
invisible wheel, doubting Countryside real, rare species bid
no good-bye

Greedy eyes desert dry.

GOOD ENERGY

Reducing fossil fuels air-drying heater, try a smart meter
convector
Clean work for renewable sector. Admit good fuel costs
cleaner than oil. Seas winds purer and cost less toil, purses
not poorer blocking big Corporates industrialized fouling
impact.
See UK's network of 1,400 renewable generators
- a praiseworthy fact.

PERMUCULTURE

Growing food on balconies, patios, school playgrounds
Hospital and church surrounds
Woman favoured for training in horticulture in cities
As in Nepal, more grain planting, uneaten chickens eating weeds
And pests, pecking, scratching, churning topsoil
while dropping manure.
Cook no hen-legs try hatching their fertilized eggs.
Obsolescence Earth's painful convalescence.

REMEDIAL

'Ann, industry then worked in a bank.
Wind in the Willows I need thank. Ratty's Riverside a cottage beside
Walk woolly alpacas in winter dank.'
''My job now, Grandad, me kicked out for a year!'
'Special Needs Ann, because you're special dear. Lovely caring kids like you always welcome here.'

SPELLBINDING

Not bindweed but vampiric blooming traps
Unlike snapdragons the skin of a reptile
Dracula orchids like spiders fly flesh saps
Aping rotten meat emitting stink that's vile.
Victorian plant kidnappers alien species from abroad
In UK for hot droughts' desiccate beech trees and sward,
Cut Ghost Orchids haunt men most?

GOOD NEWS - 1 -

Nettles dock leaves next, fish stocks hexed
Till prawns' chiton with silk cocoon mixed
Plastic decomposition fixed in 33 days.
Tackle trawler-nets, fisherman's ways.
Cut leaves in half, Kilian auric photos show
Ghostly astral outline of complete leaf
As with culling and coppicing, hunting/shooting/fishing,
Cutting down the need for grief?

GOOD NEWS - 2 -

Cattle-rustling equipment from farms stolen
Suicidal owner debts sadly swollen
Uses Nature to keep thieves at bay
Earth ramparts so stuck cars sway
Only a copper or tractor can remove.
How better criminality acts to prove
One PC guarding 450 square countryside miles
Overtime paid to overcome such illegal wiles

NATIONAL TREASURE

National Park, Yorkshire Dales, highest freshwater farm
Plus, gales, cargo-carrying canal 177 miles long
Away from commuter polluting belt.
The Waterways Museum is in Cheshire
Showing 7 main canals,
Including Devon London up to Manchester and Liverpool,
The oldest being Trent and Mersey.
Most suicide drowning in Manchester's.
Why's that?

WARNING

Pole to pole oceans' cursed plastic waste
World's curdle seas swell with souring paste
Soon more plastic than fish
Swilling toxic tides swish
To heal America in no haste.
Green seabed grass traps now microbe flakes
Feeding plankton killer wales to hakes
More love and care that's all it takes.

SPROUTS

Brussel-sprouts are green though once a year seen
European Parliament completing healthy policy of low carbon
Plus more equality as potential MPs try voters to please
And largest party in Brussels
Collect more than many a vote
While foreign factories' pollutants emote
As climates go strange,
More resistant to change...?

WISHFUL THINKING

Green Councillors not there for no selfish reason
Seeing damaging Developments as treason.
Instead, they stand for equality and fairness
Not ramming agendas down blocked throats
But on calm blue waters...
...Trusting they'll sail their organic boats.
With notions of oceans plastic-free for fishes
By setting examples seeding green wishes.

ALLEGIANCE TO EARTH

Understand global economy to preserve, people, water, land.
Assume many dream green unheard and unseen.
Daily question consumption
Challenge powers' assumption re personal privilege
And exploitation in every advanced nation.
Define progress, study watercress
Check where lettuce and coffee are grown.
Acquire fewer needs sow healthier seeds
With life-supporting deeds.

CARING KINDLY

If Gaia was a BodyShop and to its customers kind
Forget right or wrong but our clients all always right.

On seasons' rounds, earth's magnet will bind.
Each tree and leaf and bird eggs' thief at night
To every ant wasp butterfly and bee
Let's all agree in harmony

MILK OF KINDNESS

Our closed farm produces cows' feed
Using artificial insemination to breed.
We record each beast's history from birth
Listed as GM free by a Greenpeace.
Some milk and grain proteins
Cause a range of ailments
Hence dairy produce detractors.
Bring back Shire horses, forget tractors not harmed by factory farms.

UNCONQUERED

Hung on Royal Academy's wall
Hitler's pictures no winner at all.
Lorded on London city breaks,
No bombs till city breaks
WW2 for Berlin no fall.
Mother Nature won't be conquered by man's puny powers
No matter how many bouquets of cut-flowers
May sea-beds again rise for men to prize…?

CONSEQUENCES

Home-gardens no low-maintenance farms
Costly foods but no bankrupt firms of arms
Killer and killed corpses,
Fewer soldiers spoilsports
Legalised murder rehearsed in innocent wildernesses
Wildlife flee leaving the honeybee to perish in flowers
Fears fuelling all human's transcendent powers
Making more of men's messes
For uniformed corpses more caresses.

ENLIGHTENED

I'm in my own zone my best friend the telephone
Free to do my own thing since the phone doesn't ring
Birds have their wings and bees their own stings
Who needs wedding rings when Creation gives all things?
All green growth reaches for the sun
Making Light of it.

COSMIC CLASSROOM

'Ann, powerbases by implication like males,
As each complies but quails.
Mothers now join infantry's forces with widow spiders' fatal fangs
Or like beasts killing weakest cubs from foe's greedy gangs.'
'Schools demanded my compliance
Complete reliance.
Grandad, I'm no slave!
Swelling State coffers while nature gives us free offers.

MISSION MEDITATION - 1 -

'Unlimited its provisions, as we make our revisions
Life's lessons as invitations to share as man overrides
What Nature decides?

Presently your mission on earth is vailed.'
But if my Guardian Angel had emailed me
What then? My reason for being here and now?'
'What blessings Ann might messages endow?'

MISSION MEDITATION - 2 -

'Ann, answers already written elsewhere.
Ask your secret Self how to get there.'
'If life's muddy maze conflicted
Happy to merge with all higher laws
Fearless love will work with your Cause
Inwardly just discern your best advising voice – not me!
Never getting conned by owning each choice – you're free!'

THE WORLD

New National Heritage site
Vintage steam motors bringing blight
On water and land
Coal-fired fuel not banned
Plumes of smoke imprinting its might.
Every belief system riven.
Dogmas not seen as God-given.
Uncensored sea rises as lowlanders flee.
History mostly a mystery
Written in ego as if everyone should agree?

STRUGGLES

Men fighting for a better life as if blessed existence a beastly
battle though this not so for domesticated cattle yet.

Nature a vacuum abhors, ever new life Nature adores
Death fearless unless stench sensed in abattoirs.
Death by butchers saying no au revoirs, nonvegetarian by
taste,
Meat s smelly waste.

INSURANCE?

Nature's invasive, Insurers evasive, climates abrasive and
increasingly Impossible to predict. Hence financial brokers
reluctant to commit
To transactions, or donate to ecological Causes
Though evolution never pauses
Power-addicts always in arrears, riddled with entropic fears
Ageing printing white hair unlike the seasonal
coat-changers
Like Artic fox and hare.

SHY POLECATS

Rarely spotted let alone filmed yet featured In BBC TV's
Countryfile photographic competition cute cubs
Like home-counties' rare cuddly panda bears?
The shadow sides' rural beauty spots
Blighted by sneaky city invaders
With damaging drugs targeting special need kids
As local drug dealers, Society's victims
Often facing a hopeless Future.

IRONIES? Caringly recycled, carefully packed in overlarge *plastic* containers.

Finances profiting foodbanks thriving
With rare species going from bust to dust.
Man's careless domination, a global abomination
Seeking planets to corrupt
With good intentions.
Population 27b by 2100?
If Mother Nature resists belief in God
Is she an atheist, like every sod?

SIGHTED

Retired doctor birdie bewitched
By Europe's non-defunct corn bunting
Not at Winterbourne Downs Reserve.
But remote hedgerow its jangly song sounding like rattled keys –
Even in Russia signalling the West supports freedom's wings
Emberiza calandra?

Do classical terms not detected in modern dictionaries
Help non-experts love life's protesters and protectors?

FOR KEEPS?

Power potential castle's Keep BBC serves folks still fast
asleep
Sunday for wildlife and religious strife
RE and survival for plebs too deep?

'Ann, try to hold the same fistful of river water
In your right hand twice.
Or capture the cold draft from my study door
In a vice?

BIOBANK?

Cooked vegetables mediated from weeds
No matter how high hedge fund breeds
Profiteers or patents aiming to colonise seeds
If the extraordinary succeeds when LSD leads
Global economy - cows', chickens', swine's', diseases rife -
As if bodies in ice, will service
Cryonics beating a natural forest fire
For resurrecting life?

DECISIONS?

Decarbonisation decide -
So not more global pessimists deride.
Hot air overheats, profits' pundit cheats and lie
Earth not loved where do families abide?
Will electric plugs for driverless cars cause more solar
panels on new rooves as if windmills Dutch landscape mars?
How soon before each of us scared moves...to where?

FOOD BANKS?

Buying *plastic* tubes for human resuscitation,
Non-biodegradable for global digestion?
This is a paradox based on binary coding.
At least the path less travelled is centre of roads.
Roadkill fills no raptors' crops
Farmers' crops fill the crow as old cronies grumble.

'Like you, grandad. After every grumble, you tumble…!'

PESSIMISM?

Man's corporate work is earth's corruption
Obliterating destruction
Excessive foul air fumigating all exhausted parts
Unstable oxygen for earth's corruption
'You are excessively negative,' commended Mohammed
A Facebook accuser or an abuser?
Author also as negative? Those six lines above distrust?
Or are they more accurate than not – discuss disgust?

UNMOURNED?

Under motorways uncounted murdered worms
Planes and trains ruin rural beauty feeding fat firms
Nature killed for cash gains, remunerated by deaths' stains.
All life let live including germs, less pills more sunlight
before ill
Herbs grown indoors, consuming nutritious prawns.
Robots mowing lawns, wherever now the wild grazing
fawns?

WILD WAYS

Wild killer pets uncensored unnamed
Feral feline tabby queens feisty caught untamed.
No trapped violin spiders petrified.
Lethal serpents prettified,
Also, no dull raptor glider as kaleidoscopic diver
kingfisher's flash,
Warrior autumn trees dismiss died-back ash other plants
avoid. Furtive fungi as fairy folk,
Like Creation Spirituality,
Not a joke?

ECCONOMY V AUTONOMY?

Diversity biological adversity daily
116 miles of rain forest felled gaily
Using energy efficiently
Implementing practical sufficiency
Solar farms floating on rainfalls' reservoirs
Before bidding whole health our au revoirs
We unsuited to a biosphere's mechanics
On laws of thermodynamics
And ecology
With no apology.
Hope like energy fraternal
Eternal

PATHWAYS

We human bridges prevent road-kills
Yet rural transport rings no tills.

Grass supported wildflowers bereft of bees
Royal sweet jelly wax honey
Planet Venus gifted
As so corals' secrets safeguarded by the Lucius Trust
Together with Schumacher
Followers all uplifted!
Beware venomous world's boil
Delivering dust
All feared incendiaries bust.

HOLLOW SORROW?

'Only dead creatures on roads
Not on country jogs
Pork on dinner plates never found
Dead forest hogs
In our house all sorts of poor things somehow, dies.
Moths butterflies wasps spiders flies
Grandad, don't want to find you dead.'

'Ann darling, me as tasty road-kill? My Soul long fled!'

CLINGERS

Pollen spores in extinct mammals' guts' wee meteors
Winter chill kills 70% of dormice snores
No squirrels of nut allergy
Blood sucked by cat fleas.
No displeased demented pets consented
Till cider vinegar applied to irritating mites
Ringworm needing a good scratch before more bites

Ivies, choking passive trees, parasites?

MARBLES

'Ann, think maltesers, found like gender-specific boji stones
One held each hand
But also found strewn over Kanas ground
Like moqui or shaman earth stones, chakras scanned'
'Stops me getting giddy not all over the place like a
busy-Lizzy?'
'Sandstone, iron surrounds, honeycomb structures
See endoscopy probing ants' mounds?'

EXHALTIONS

Nothing more exhausting than grief.
Let autumn leaves be your brief
No natural possession, super life's progression,
Holy cows don't cry over beef.
Meat-eating carcinogenic, mind's limitation's academic,
Digesting facts as if they're all flawless
Like fracking and mining so men bore less -
Pond-like gravel-pits sport fish and willow tits?

KINDLY TIMELY

Penguin's cosmic clock chick stuck in oil-slick
Feathers cleansed by carer so bird's tail can flick.
From adult colony braking ranks, making poor fisherman
feel royal
2000-mile swim each anniversary gave deep thanks
Annual rewarding returns to clean coast
To celebrate his birdlife
Not a ghost.
Sincere love's no need to boast.

NATURE'S CALENDAR - 1 -

King of Fishers in blue and gold naughty birds
Won't do what they're told
Can't wait to be taught
Eat fast what you've caught
Swift colourful streakers when too cold.

But beware unwary fish for headfirst in one swish
Swallowed whole into orange belly
Rivers its best water Deli.

NATURE'S CALENDAR - 2 -

Baby roe deer they love to play
You can see them both night and day.

In woods if you met treat deer as a pet
Why be sad if it ran away?

February stag's antlers shed,
Some on hunters' trophy wall.
But by spring all ready
For the mating brawl.

NATURE'S CALENDAR - 3 -

Otters in rivers are so rare
Quick to see one if then they're there
They splash swim and fish kids often will wish
To see them but go if you stare. A pup can be tamed.
By an author one named.
Ann got book from grandad's archive.
Tarquin will survive.

NATURE'S CALENDAR - 4 -

Harvest mouse with two big black eyes,
Of all the mice the smallest size.
Long tail its fifth limb, green grasses its gym.
Hearing corn harvester it flees for life.
With her teeth, Mrs Mouse shreds grasses
To weave into a nest.
Weighing only 6g on stalks it can rest.

NATURE'S CALENDAR - 5 -

Tawny owl big claws eyes and ears
That's the bird the harvest mouse fears.
When hunting no hoot so mice do not scoot
If mice escapes let's give three cheers?
Not cute like smaller owls.
Frequent roadkill at night
On wrong branch mobbed by songbirds
That perch their Right.

NATURE'S CALENDAR - 6 -

One body 6 eyes, 2 wings. Peacock butterfly never stings
Like bees it loves flowers. Not in heavy showers.
Much sunshine and happiness this brings.
Mum's eggs hatch when young caterpillars,
By nettles not stung

Photographed on butterfly wings from around the world,
Markings show letter A-Z and number, 1-9.

NATURE'S CALENDAR - 7 -

Sea parrot puffin bird a clown
Clumsy walker often falls down
Not easily found they nest underground
On island clifftops far from town.
See waddling parents stumble in July,
14 sandeels in their beak
Twitchers say, 'Oopsie!
For birds that can't speak.
Tough, before falls
They utter strange greeting calls.

NATURE'S CALENDAR - 8 -

Badgers tiptoe out at twilight watch
But don't touch sharp teeth can bite.
They dig up earthworms the quickest one squirms
Back into the soil out of sight
Like hedgehogs accused so spreading TB,
Will pogroms, ethnic cleansing and culling human fears
And prejudices lulling, discernments dulling,
Delaying unbiased mulling?

NATURE'S CALENDAR - 9 -

Big eyes and ears twitchy nose chased by dogs
Off it goes swerving as if eyes behind. Being solitary difficult to find.
Seeming asleep, hares off on toes
And on long legs can leap
The mountain hare feeding up for snowfalls
Its fur turning white
Again, not easy to sight.

NATURE'S CALENDAR - 10 -

Married mute swans mates life-long
Only hissing when faced with strife
Their cygnets in nest, they, needing rest,
Warmed by dad and wife.
Projected by Queen, black and white.
No colour-bar by Right
In Saint-Saens' *Carnival of Animals* suite.
Classical musical treat.
Tree-rings outlasted by stones feathers by hollow bones.

NATURE'S CALENDAR - 11 -

Protected climbers pine martens leap trees
In their rich fur coat, they don't freeze
As small birds they catch. As athletes no match
Of weasels' antics, the most agile these
After red squirrels when starving
Sharp teeth and claws for carving
Like the wildcat.
Both rare in the wilds threatened habitat.

NATURE'S CALENDAR - 12 -

Highland wildcat hides with its mate
Often hunted that was their fate
A few left to roam
High woodlands their home.
Not cold in thick fur snow not their fate
Tabby-like not missing household vetting. Or petting.
Cats in every continent go-getting.
No fear of death - so far, less fretting.

HOUSETRAINED?

How many creatures have you seen?
Some wash behind their ears some less keen
To blow their own nose
Or wash behind toes
Which creatures don't like to stay clean?

Pigs in thick mud like to wallow
Where mummy pigs go piglets follow
Pink noses smell roots
Nibble farmer's boots.

CATS AND DOGS

Licking cats nuzzle into fur
Love to be stroked and love to purr
But scratched by sharp paws we risk getting red sores.

Cats or dogs which do you prefer? Dogs swim
jumping in pools
Biting bones sharp teeth their tools
Ann, only a fool thinks cats can't be trained in any school.

EMBEDDED

Bedbugs hide in cracks, sipping blood their lifelong
Snacks often transported on second-hand antiques
Like old bedding bought in boutiques.
Though the size of an apple pip
Their colour darkens after one sip
Leaving a nasty red bump till next victim triggers a jump.

Nature's editor –
Man, earth's exploitative predator.

LIVED-REVERSED

Devils are never in short supply
But Tasmanian Devils are killed or die
So saved to live in cages to let them live for ages.
As if they can become holy saintly.
An anthropomorphic sentiment held faintly
Based on wishful thinking, till to their wild habitat linking,
Despite reputation stinking.

DELUGES

Ann dreamed plastic being liquefied the world's pessimists
defied.
Mixed with human excrement and other ingredients to
complement
Spread along earth's sea-beds, plankton better thriving
Krill multiply surviving
Improving the food-chain upwards from life's watery womb
Saving us from doom.
Longer than MU and Atlantis now in the oceans' tomb.

MIXED MESSAGES

Ice-caps melting quicker, livestock getting sicker,
Human longevity increasing, healthy air decreasing.
Sea-levels rising, ecologists advising
Ozone levels shrinking, coastal areas sinking
Ann constantly grinning
As if optimism had no Beginning
And dead ends don't exist,
While natural Survival she'll assist?
Eating Organic, resisting panic, materials recycled, not
getting manic.

PODS

Encrusted crucible of consciousness in human form
Each seed of surprising life bursts into a swarm
Africa's jungles savannas bleak teaming soils
Spawned mankind for survival's toils
On lowest rope-ladder rung Souls sprung
Were still so young
Millennia of multiple experiences pending
Life as love mixed learning is never ending.

STELLA MUSES

In aether nothing's ever empty
Unseen's pregnant with plenty
Sunset Mars blue before mankind flew
Or Queen of Night aliens might frighten
Asronaughts exploring through sciences
Returned poets enraptured by cosmic alliances
No created redundancy. All breeds amazing abundancy
Pioneering out-of-body spaced-out séances
Looking for life elsewhere as here's
EVERYWHERE!

COMPOUNDS

Life's needs downloaded elements online as carbon
hydrogen
Magic crystals as oversouls plus sulphur phosphorus
nitrogen
Buried gems by their own Master guided
All encouraging growth faster as vibrations decided
Inwardly as outwardly can heal or destroy
Till for Old Soul Atlanteans 'Land Ahoy!'
Devas had crafted a homebound bouncing buoy.

DEVAS

Of the uncountable physical homes
Earth the favoured one for gnomes
Attracting those the planet would save
Dryads comfort woods so they behave
Sometimes healing wounded trees.
Naiads or nymphs with ondines these
Not forgetting fresh air sylphs
Salamanders in log fires deep meditators ease
And psychic researchers please.

NATURE'S HEALERS - 1 -

Father Fire cooked earth's microscopic ancestors
Air and water are Earth's enthused spirit investors
Fired up it enlivens all beings blood red
To bake bread and break bread, flames fairly spread
This often-unseen fuel. Not cool or cruel
Offering light even as lives are shed for fire nothing's ever dead.

NATURE'S HEALERS - 2 -

'What makes water wet?' asked Ann once more
'Good question,' said Grandad, 'Why not explore?'
In Holy Wells church bells heard in fountains
Flowing like bloodstreams in rainbows and mountains
Cleansing as with tears dripping in oceans
Honing focus, if not hocus pokus
Busting pipes if stuck
In stale notions.

NATURE'S HEALERS - 3 -

'This world here before Big Bang burst?
Man's conceit put Earth first
Of all elements from four to seven
Long before Ann, let alone heaven
Mummy Earth not Daddy Sun the centre of the universe
Mind brainwashed by power freaks what could be worse
Turning prayerful plea into a curse?'

CONGERING MIRACLES?

Controversy re-considered; fairies photographed in
Cottingley –
On a ley-line? - were accredited by Arthur Conan Doyle
Discredited by the girl photographers.
Yet the young cousins said they had seen real fairies
Exeter University researching how to contact
The Fairy Kingdom
Although all but one of the photographs
Were claimed as fakes.

AUTONOMOUS

Harvesting water from air
Ice on the moon, dry riverbeds on Mars
Weather-control said to be possible
Ann claimed everything's possible.
Buy a new pipe for Grandad and arrange a birthday party?
One meant getting wet, so she ordered, 'Rain STOP!'
It didn't
Drizzle
Ann resigned, made up her own mind!

HOGS

Ann's houseplants she greets like cats and dogs
Not so much at Pets' Corner
She'd rather hug wild hogs and study winged fairies
Dancing on rotten logs!
Missions. Missionaries. Pioneers. Reformers trusting kinship
appears
Elsewhere as well as hereabouts
Invisible vibrations pulsating everywhere
Except when prodded.
Nowhere there - where's there?

ELUSIVE SOLUTIONS

Truth hard to pull as sheep's wool
Men's wallets millions spewing out gelt on space
After spreading trillions of dosh in wages
Killing life on his own planet base for ages
Mindless murders as if trees would poison their own roots
As mankind their fruits. Nero? Noah? Nature's next hero?

ON EARTH PAN SPEAKS

Adapted from records held
at the Findhorn Foundation Scotland by

CHRISTOPHER GILMORE

Mob: 07837 971 408
www.ChristopherGilmore.co.uk

ON EARTH PAN SPEAKS

THE SOUND COMES FROM THE TREES AND SHRUBS AND IS HEARD TO WANDER.)
THE AUDIENCE WILL ENTER THE ROYAL BOTANIC GARDEN BY THE EAST GATE.

EACH PERSON WILL RECEIVE A PROGRAMME AND, IF REQUESTED,
A FOLDING CANVAS STOOL.
THIS IS TO BE OUTDOOR WALKABOUT THEATRE.

WHILE THE PRESENT VERSION IS TO FIT THE GROUNDS OF THE ROYAL BOTANICAL GARDEN, EDINBURGH,
IT COULD BE ADAPTED TO SUIT
OTHER BEAUTUFUL GARDENS SUCH AS BODANT GARDEN IN WALES
OR POSSIBLY
IN AN ARBORETUM, NATURE RESERVE
A TATTON PARK OR OTHER SUITABLE VENUES

PAN PIPES ARE HEARD PLAYING.

STAGE ONE: <u>THE HORSE CHESTNUT TREE</u>

(THE AUDIENCE IS ASSEMBLED UNDER THE CHESTNUT TREE NEAR THE EAST GATE. HIGH UP AND HIDDEN IN ITS BRANCHES, THE PAN PIPES COME TO REST. SILENCE.

AS THE MUSIC FINISHES, <u>LAWSON</u> APPEARS AMONG THE WAITING PEOPLE. HE POINTS TO THE TRUNK OF THE CHESTNUT TREE. (687099)

LAWSON Have you noticed the 'hieroglyphics'? On that tree? Maybe they mean something ... (pause). Let's start with our ancestors. They used to worship trees. In fact, they'd try to explain all existence, not by science like us, but by stories. With fairy tales. After all, everything in nature, from the seahorse to the chestnut tree, likes to tell its story.

(PAUSE).

Will you all look at this horse chestnut tree .... for ....say ....thirty seconds. Let's just absorb this tree ....in silent contemplation....

(HE GESTURES FOR THEM TO SIT. SILENCE)

So much for eyes. Now, like ancient children in the winter of the Dark Ages, let's close our eyes. (PAUSE). Once upon a time, where that tree now stands, there stood a little boy. In one hand he held three seeds. In the other he held a meat skewer. A string was tied through the handle. He wanted to play conkers, but the chestnuts were harder than he expected. As he struggled to pierce them, the smallest conker fell to the ground, rolled away and hid trembling under a leaf.

After two weeks, the hidden chestnut felt safe. Cautiously, it released a sound, a small sound, beyond the reach of little boys' ears. This was the signal, though to the nature spirits. They were being called to help. They worked for years. Tirelessly. They built up, bit by bit, a beautiful tree. Each root, each shoot, stem, leaf and flower, year in and year out, until the tree had its wish fulfilled. Fully grown, it lit up the good garden with its candelabra of shimmering white blossoms.

In celebration, all the invisible workers vibrate, like busy bees. Each individual's note harmonises so that, all together, they make a joyful chord. This sound we can receive. It is the gift of scent. Thus, as the nature spirits hymn their thanksgiving for this beautiful green giant, we receive the gift of their music, as perfume.

It's not Spring now but imagine the scent. Whatever we imagine must exist. Breathe in deeply and you will smell the scent of the next spring...NOW.

(PAUSE)

LAWSON (contd.) How much of that fairy story seems possible? Look at that tree again. Examine it and empathise...

(A LONG PAUSE)

Like all of us, this tree has inside itself the desire to stretch and grow. Not just volcanoes, all creation seems to have this urge to rise. Hills wish to be mountains; shrubs, trees; seeds, flowers; water, floods; floods, clouds.

And if all of this sounds too fanciful, might I mention that not only am I a Botanist well versed in the life sciences but, at the moment, I'm engaged with astrophysics, delving into black holes and the like. Way up out there, old Mother Nature doesn't use her mirror so much. Life is more mysterious still. Only glimpsed through a glass, darkly...

(HE MIMES A TELESCOPE.)

What visions await us all....

(SUDDENLY, HE JERKS HIS HAND UP AS THOUGH TO GIVE THE NAZI SALUTE. INSTEAD, HE SNAPS BACK ALL BUT HIS INDEX FINGER, LEAVING IT POINTING TO THE SKY.)

We scientists name five regions up there-troposphere, tropopause, stratosphere, ionosphere and....the unknown. The moon was once unknown. Yet the Zen Buddhists said, centuries ago: "A finger is needed to point to the moon but once the moon is recognised, we need not trouble ourselves with a finger ...."

(HE STOPS POINTING, RELUCTANTLY LOWERS HIS HAND.)

Agreeing modestly, some physicists now go further. "There is no known reason why ...." "they say, "why ...."

(HE AGAIN JABS THE SKY WITH HIS FINGER.)

"...This finger is not pointing through five different dimensions at the same moment." (PAUSE) Scientists name five regions up there. The mystics name five celestial bodies....

(HE POINTS AT HIS OWN CHEST.)

.... in HERE. A Chinese puzzle box filled with the interlocking bodies of the Etheric, Mental, Causal, Astral and the Physical.

(HE THUMPS HIS CHEST.)

Five levels without, Five bodies within. Five senses. Or are there SIX? Two eyes. Or are there THREE? Only mathematicians need to count. Those who know don't even need their mind. Soul, in its natural state, is not only happy but WISE.

Then what is our natural state? Well I've been studying many paths through many lifetimes. Even as a simple fish I was studying the angelfish. It made me yearn to fly.

(HE TAKES OUT A SMALL BOOK.)

Geoffrey Hodson, in 'THE KINGDOM OF THE FAERIE', explains that Pan, the best known of the nature spirits, always manifest during an upsurge of earth awareness. I hope 'The Friends of the Earth' are not affronted by this thought. (READING FROM BOOK) "Pan was on the downward arc when his cycle and that of humanity touched on another in the past." During my Greek spell on earth, actually. (READING) "In the future, when the corresponding point is reached in the next cycle, Pan will be on the path of return." That is, during our present lifetime. NOW!

(HE CLOSES THE BOOK AND GESTURE FOR THE AUDIENCE TO RISE.) Shall we follow that path...? Whatever you wish to see you will see .... with one eye or another. Let us all see....Let us all read aloud.

(HE LEADS THE WAY, RECITING, WITH THE AUDIENCE WORDS IN THEIR PROGRAMME NOTES.)

What was he doing, the great god Pan,
Down by the reeds by the river?
Spreading ruin and scattering ban
Splashing and paddling with hoof of a goat,
And breaking the golden lilies afloat
With the dragon fly on the river.

He tore out a reed, the great god Pan,
From the deep cool bed of the river:
The limpid water, turbidly ran
And the broken lilies a-dying lay,
And the dragon fly had fled away,
Ere he brought it out of the river.

High on the shore sat the great god Pan,
While turbidly flowed the river:
And hacked and hewed as a great god can
With his hard bleak steel at the patient reed,

Till there was not a sign of a leaf indeed
To prove it fresh from the river.

(DURING THE THIRD VERSE OF A MUSICAL INSTRUMENT 'BY ELIZABETH BARRETT BROWNING, LAWSON IS JOINED BY A STRANGE DARK BROWN VOICE

IT SEEMS TO TRAVEL THROUGH THE UNDERGROWTH.

(MEANWHILE, THE AUDIENCE IS BEING LED TO THE NEXT STAGE. LAWSON NOW SINGS:)

(Singing)
He cut it short did the great god Pan
(How tall it stood in the river)
Then drew the pith like a heart of a man
Steadily from the outside ring
And notched the poor dry empty thing
In holes, as he sat by the river.

This is the way, laughed the great god Pan
(laughed as he sat by the river)
"The only way, since gods began
To make sweet music they could succeed"
Then dropping his mouth to a hole in the reed
He blew in power by the river.

LAWSON (singing) Sweet, sweet, sweet, O Pan!
Piercing sweet by the river!
Blinding sweet O great god Pan!
The sun on the hill forgot to die
And the lilies revived and the dragonfly
Come back to the dream on the river.
(THE LAST VERSE IS A DUET, LAWSON AND AN UNIDENTIFIED DARK BROWN VOICE).

Yet half a beast is the great god Pan
To laugh as he sits by the river,
Making a poet out of a man,
The true gods sigh for the cost and pain -
For the reed that grows never more again
As a reed with reeds in the river.
(THE AUDIENCE IS NOW AT THE NEXT STAGE)

STAGE TWO: <u>THE WATERFALL IN THE ROCK GARDEN</u>

(THE AUDIENCE IS NOW STANDING, ABOVE THE ACTION, LOOKING DOWN)

LAWSON As a young boy, Tesla, the electrical inventor, knew that one day he would harness the power of the Niagara Falls. In an old book, he'd come across an engraving of these gigantic waterfalls, many moons before he was a scientist or knew, indeed, that he would visit that Never-Never Land, America.

Our story also starts and ends, happily, with a waterfall and wishing well. For this is the story of another scientific mystic, Robert Ogilvie Crombie, known as Roc.

Since his twenties, Roc lived in the same flat in Edinburgh. He was someone for whom schooling never stopped. His library contained seven thousand books. Like myself, he never ceased to explore: Greek myths, photography, electronics, chemistry, physics and many other disciplines with an objective search for truth.

Further, he always sought to confirm his experiments with experience.

To his friends he was often as enigmatic as mist: still, yet elusive; playful, yet timelessly wise. Yet, in human terms, it was alone that Roc partook

of his greatest relaxation - wandering through the beautiful Royal Botanic Garden.
Imagine this is a Fairy Glen and that I am Roc....

(HE STARTS TO CHANGE INTO THE PART OF ROC)

We are near the little seaside town of Rosemarkie and the year is 1974. Roc is revisiting an old childhood haunt. A lovely day. While looking at the waterfall, suddenly, on the flat stone in front of him, three gnomes appear.

(LAWSON HAS NOW BECOME THE 67-YEAR-OLD ROC.
HE SPEAKS NOW WITH A GENTLE EDINBURGH LILT. IN THIS NEXT SCENE, WE DO NOT SEE THE GNOMES, ONLY HEAR THEIR VOICES. ROC WATCHES THEM WITH DELIGHT.)

1st GNOME (sound over) My, you have grown up.
ROC What do you mean?
2nd GNOME (sound over) We remember a little boy coming here, long ago in our time.
3rd GNOME (sound over) It WAS you and aren't you glad your wish was granted?
ROC (puzzled) What wish?
1st GNOME Don't you remember dropping a penny in the wishing well and wishing you could see....

(THEY ARE HEARD TO GIGGLE)

2nd GNOME And bubbles rose from the pebbles on the bottom of the well, which meant that your wish would be granted.
ROC That must be...yes, I remember now ... must be all of sixty-three years ago. I was four. LOOK...!

(SUDDENLY, AT THE TOP OF THE GLEN, ABOVE THE AUDIENCE, THREE CHILDREN APPEAR. THEY SOUND RATHER LIKE THE

GNOMES JUST HEARD BUT ARE OBVIOUS HUMANS. THEY RUN LAUGHING AND LAND ON THE FLAT STONE. THEY ENJOY TEASING THE YOUNGEST CHILD,

WTHI THROBERT. THEY SING:)

WISHING WELL

ALL 3

ONE, TWO, THREE
SING A LITTLE SPELL,
DROP YOUR PENNY
IN THE WELL. (the BOY does so)
MAKE A WISH AND MAKE IT BOLD
LET ME SEE
(They close their eyes, holding their noses)

BOY — LOTS OF CANDY AND GOLD!

ALL 3 — O WISHING WELL, WISHING WELL
WHAT SHALL WE WISH?

ROC — WHEN I WAS A WORM
I WISHED TO BE A FISH

ALL 3 — ONE, TWO, THREE
SING A LITTLE SPELL, DROP YOUR PENNY
IN THE WELL. (The GIRL does so)
MAKE A WISH AND MAKE IT BOLD
LET ME BE (they close their eyes, hold their noses)

GIRL — NEVER UGLY OR OLD.

ALL 3 — O WISHING WELL, WISHING WELL
MY WISH BE HEARD.

ROC — WHEN I WAS A FISH
I LONGED TO BE A BIRD.

ALL 3 — ONE, TWO, THREE
SING A LITTLE SPELL,
DROP YOUR PENNY

IN THE WELL. (ROC does so)
MAKE A WISH AND MAKE IT BOLD
LET ME SEE (they close their eyes, holding their noses)

ROC (after a long, agonised pause) SECRETS CANNA'BE TOLD.

GIRL No' fair, no' fair! We told OURS!

BOY Tell us, Robbie, or I'll give ye a wee clout....
(THE YOUNG ROC SHAKES HIS HEAD)
Then I'll give ye a BIG clout... stupid ...
(HE CLOUTS THE YOUNG ROC)

ROC (holding his ground) I'm no telling. Nobody. Secret.

GIRL Be fair, Robert. Tell just ME!

(YOUNG ROC SHAKES HIS HEAD)

BOY Then Liz an' me, we won't play with you. See how you like that, getting LOST....

GIRL Leave him all alone?
(THE YOUNG ROC, SMILING, SHAKES HIS HEAD. HE'S HOPING FOR OTHER FRIENDS)

BOY He's screwy. Come on, Liz...
(THEY LEAVE HIM. THE YOUNG ROC IS NOT UNHAPPY.
HE DOES NOT FEEL ALONE.)

ROC (singing)
O WISHING WELL, WISHING WELL
DEEP ARE YOUR SPRINGS
WHEN I AM A MAN
I'LL WISH TO BE ON WINGS.
(YOUNG AND OLD ROC NOW REPEAT THE LAST TWO LINES, SINGING TOGETHER).

ROCs (together)
WHEN I AM A MAN
I'LL WISH TO BE ON WINGS.

(LAWSON NOW DROPS THE CHARACTERISTICS OF ROC. AS LAWSON, HE POINTS TO THE YOUNG BOY BY THE WATER.)

LAWSON There's a thought. A wish is just a thought. But a thought is a force. Just as much as a child is a force. Or a Church is a force. Or a bubble. They are all spirit forces that can make moulds for the future, by wishing. In fact, physics has become so sophisticated now, searching for a theorem which not only incorporates the quantum and relativity theories, but also includes us, or the OBSERVER, as an ingredient. After all, is a mirror a mirror before we look at it? And when we see ourselves reflected in a spoon and we are upside-down, which way round is the truth, then? How is it that we can see through a pane of glass but not through a brick wall when they're both made from the same thing, SAND? So that when we "hold, as 't'were, a mirror up to Nature, "perhaps we're looking not just at Blake's grain of sand; not just as Christ's mustard seed; but also deep into our own atom of reflective soul. This could suggest that the cosmos is a scattered shattering of countless similar tiny fragments, each a scrap splintered from God's giant two-way looking glass.

Maybe, this jigsaw-puzzle picture will not be complete until all the scattered fragments are again united. Thus whatever our wish when staring at our reflection in the well, we yearn to be nearer the creative force, the ALL.

Was this Roc's secret wish as a child?

As the word 'panic' derives from the name of Pan, so the word 'wish' derives from the ancient

name for god, HU. Thus, hue and cry. To be god-inclined was to be HU-ish. This was the original spelling for the word WISH. Without a wishbone, no bird can fly…!
The word 'HU', OR god, can be chanted as of old and with your permission, that's what we shall be doing, shortly, raising the vibrations by sound.
After this, when you next open your eyes, I'll be leading you towards Roc's favourite tree, Zelkova Caripinifola, the Tree of Life. By then, it will be Midsummer's Eve, a time very special to the Nature Spirits. Pan will be present, as always, whether or not we see him.

Now in chanting the ancient word for god, HU, we can still raise the vibrations according to the quality of the contributions. Cause and effect.

Whether or not you are a mystic or a cynic, your very presence is a contribution, perhaps just a passive one.

Yes, so what I'm suggesting is participation, on the very deepest level, you and I chanting, together. As you close your eyes, I suggest you let your attention come to rest on the pineal gland. That's to be found HERE. (HE POINTS TO HIS OWN) This is the two-way mirror, the third eye, the keyhole of the cosmos. With sound we can ease the door more open, by using the word. In the beginning was the sound and the sound was HU. (Starting the chant) HUUU....

(HE LEADS THE AUDIENCE IN THE CHANTING. AFTER ABOUT TWO MINUTES OF THIS, HE LEADS THE PEOPLE TO THE NEXT STAGE IN SILENCE.

THIS IS A BEAUTIFULTHREE MINUTE WALK THROUGH THE ROCK GARDENS).

STAGE THREE: <u>THE HEATH GARDEN</u>

(AS THEY APPROACH THE TREE OF LIFE, LAWSON AGAIN ADOPTS THE CHARACTERISTICS OF ROC.

AS THE AUDIENCE GETS NEARER, THEY ARE SUDDENLY STOPPED BY A VOICE. IT SEEMS TO COME FROM THE TRUNK OF THE TREE.)

TREE Afraid?

(THE AUDIENCE IS ENCOURAGED TO HOLD ITS GROUND, TO SIT AND WITNESS THE FOLLOWING FROM A DISTANCE. TO ENCOURAGE THE SEMBLANCE OF TELEPATHIC COMMUNICATION, IT IS SUGGESTED THAT THE NEXT TWO DUOLOGUES ARE PRE-RECORDED. THE BODY LANGUAGE OF ROC WILL SYNCHRONISE WITH HIS OWN CONTRIBUTIONS.

FEARLESSLY, ROC APPROACHES THE TREE AND, FASCINATED, STUDIES THE TRUNK OF THE TREE.)

ROC (sound over) Strong, powerful, and... strange...these markings on the bark....about 14 inches high. It's a form... slightly sinister....with horns, like a faun. What striking eyes! Now it's a mist. And now.... emerging.... the entity itself. about my height and broad, too. Fierce, challenging eyes...

TREE (sound over) Afraid?

ROC	No.
TREE	Would you have been so drawn to me if you'd seen me before?

(ROC GOES NEARER TO THE TREE)

ROC	Yes, I think so.
TREE	Will you touch the tree as you have always done, aware this time that you are doing it THROUGH me?

(ROC PLACES HIS HAND NEAR THE TRUNK)

ROC	A strong field, like electrified mist. (Touching the bark) The usual strong flow of energy.
TREE	Now lean your back against the tree, again THROUGH ME.
ROC	(doing so) A strange, warming energy.
TREE	You find me odd. Not what you expected. You are not repulsed?
ROC	I'm disconcerted. But I love this tree and you are the tree. You are not evil.
TREE	I am neither good nor evil. The Tree of Life. I am what you make of me.

(ROC IS ABOUT TO EMBRACE THE TREE WHEN HE SEES SOMEONE COMING. HE SWERVES INTO A MORE USUAL POSTURE.

A LONG-HAIRED YOUTH WITH A SKETCH-PAD, APPROACHES THE TREE. ROC AFFECTS NORMALITY,

NOT DRAWING NOW, OR LATER, ANY UNDUE NOTICE FROM THIS YOUNG ARTIST.)

ROC (ever so over-ordinary) Good afternoon.

ARTIST Hi!

(ON ROC'S LEFT-HAND SIDE, THE ARTIST STUDIES THE TREE, WONDERING WHETHER OR NOT TO SKETCH IT. MEANWHILE, ROC KEEPS STARING BETWEEN HIM AND AT SOMETHING ON HIS RIGHT. IT IS PAN. AS YET WE CANNOT SEE HIM. TO SUGGEST CLOSE COMMUNICATION ROC AND PAN'S VOICE ARE ON PLAY-BACK.)

PAN (sound over) Seeing this aspect of the tree's spirit has made no difference?

ROC (sound over) No.

(HE CHECKS ON THE ARTIST. THEY EXCHANGE DISTANT BUT NOT UNFRIENDLY SIGNALS AS THE YOUTH, SITTING CROSS-LEGGED ON THE GRASS, STARTS TO SKETCH THE TREE OF LIFE)

(To the unseen Pan) The energy field of the tree is unchanged...

(ROC CHECKS THE ARTIST AGAIN. ALL IS WELL. HE IS SKETCHING AWAY WITH HIS PENCIL, UNAWARE OF ANY STRANGE HAPPENINGS.)

You said THIS aspect of the tree's spirit - meaning he has others?

PAN The form in which he shows himself...

(QUICK AS LIGHTNING, A CREATURE IS JUST SEEN, AS IT FLASHES PAST FROM ONE BUSH INTO ANOTHER.)

ROC (unrecorded) A faun!

(THE ARTIST LOOKS UP. ROC QUICKLY DISMISSES HIS CURIOUS GAZE, SHRUGGING SHOULDERS AND WHISTLING IN AN OVER-RELAXED, HAPPY MANNER. IT WORKS. THE ARTIST CONTINUES TO WORK SKETCHING.)

PAN (still sound over) It is suited to the occasion. It has a purpose.

ROC (sound over) To test my reaction? Or to disconcert me?

PAN (smiling) Perhaps a bit of both. Your reaction was good.

(ROC STARES AT WHERE HE SAW THE FAUN FLASH BY)

ROC (recorded) I cannot wish to see a nature spirit and immediately do so ... (aloud, earnestly) However HARD I try!

(THE ARTIST LOOKS UP)

ARTIST What? Oh, just letting go, man ... then it's not hard at all...

(HE NOW SKETCHES WITH A NEW VIGOUR)

Like to watch me...?

ROC (aloud) Later perhaps, when we're finished.

ARTIST What?

ROC (quickly) The sketch. When it's finished, thank you...

(AGAIN ENGROSSED, THE ARTIST SHRUGS IN A GOOD-NATURED WAY AND CONTINUES TO DRAW THE TREE.)

PAN (sound over) It is done from our side - when it is right for you have this heightened vision or when a particular entity wishes to become visible to you.

(THE FAUN SKIPS PAST, FROM BUSH TO BUSH. ROC IS UNCERTAIN THAT HE REALLY SAW SOMETHING.)

ROC (sound over) How is it done?

PAN (as before) Imagine a theatre with a large stage....

ROC (surprised) How do you know about man's places of entertainment?

PAN I am everywhere. Have you forgotten how I sat in the empty seat beside you at a performance of A Midsummer Night's Dream at the Edinburgh Festival?

(AGAIN, ANOTHER STREAK OF FAUN AS IT HIDES BEHIND MORE BUSHES.)

ROC Yes, you liked the little Welshman's Puck.

PAN It was acceptable!

(THE FAUN POKES HIS FACE OUT, NODS, GRINS AND VANISHES. ROC GAPES. THE FAUN REAPPEARS.)

PAN The stage is in darkness...

(THE FAUN PLACES A HAND OVER HIS EYES AND DISAPPEARS. ROC ALSO CLOSES HIS EYES, HIS FACE STILL INCLINING TO WHERE THE FAUN WAS SEEN TO VANISH LAST.)

PAN It is thronged with people....

(ROC LOOKS AT THE AUDIENCE.)

....but you cannot see them because of the darkness.

(LIKE THE FAUN BEFORE HIM, ROC PLACES HIS RIGHT HAND OVER HIS CLOSED EYES.)

This symbolises your lack of sensitivity.

(ROC PLACES THE OTHER HAND OVER HIS EYES.)

A narrow-beam spotlight picks out one of them and he immediately becomes visible in this way...

(FULL OF PLAYFUL VANITY, THE FAUN DANCES ROUND AND ROUND THE NEARBY PINE TREE.)

Similarly, lights could pick out a group or the whole stage could be lit. The light symbolises your heightened senses.

(AS THE LIGHT SEEMS TO GET BRIGHTER, KURMOS, THE FAUN, VANISHES FROM SIGHT.)

It is a rough analogy, but it may answer your question.

ROC It does. The lights are controlled by some being on your side, I take it.

PAN Yes.

ROC Therefore, I can't select the entities I am to see or when. But I am aware of and can communicate with your subjects.

PAN Of course, you can do this at any time, though you may only be able to see us on special occasions.

(AT ANOTHER VANTAGE POINT, KURMOS POPS INTO VIEW, WAVES AND VANISHES. ROC GIVES OUT A REAL CRY. IN ITS TURN, THIS STARTLES THE ARTIST.)

ARTIST It's ready, yeah...

(HE CROSSES TO ROC, HOLDING OUT THE SKETCH-PAD. AFTER A FEW STEPS, KURMOS FOLLOWS THE ARTIST, IMITATING HIS GAIT, UNSEEN BY THE YOUTH, WHO THRUSTS THE DRAWING AT ROC, PROUDLY.)

ROC (unrecorded, approvingly) Ah, YES!

(KURMOS STANDS ON TIPTOE TO GET A LOOK. ROC STARES AT HIM QUIZZICALLY)

ARTIST Like the faun?
ROC I was just looking at him!
ARTIST Just came to me. Cool.
ROC Pardon? (LOOKS AT PICTURE) Very lifelike, yes. How on earth...?
ARTIST Imagination. See you....

(PLEASED WITH ROC'S ADMIRATION, HE STROLLS OFF LOOKING FOR ANOTHER TARGET FOR HIS PENCIL.)

PAN (sound over) Don't forget that all the great arts contain, behind them, eternal reality. The spiritual teachings. And in some cases, the basic truths of the ancient wisdom and is a source of the great esoteric teachings, though concealed in symbolic terms.

(ROC CHECKS THERE ARE NO HUMANS NEAR)

ROC (unrecorded) But so many despise art and despite their boasted intellect, take the true reality for imagination and believe that the illusionary is the real.

PAN (heard smiling) Like Plato's men in the cave, turning their backs on the truth and taking the shadows of the wall as reality.

ROC (unrecorded) Pan talking of Plato!

(ROC LAUGHS. A CITY GENT, WITH FOLDED 'FINANCIAL TIMES APPEARS. HE LOOKS AT ROC. ROC QUICKLY TURNS HIS LAUGHTER TO A BOUT OF COUGHING. THE GENT NODS, CURTLY, AND CONTINUES, NOT HEARING PAN'S REPLY.)

PAN (sound over) After all, I am Greek and proud of our philosophers.

(AS THE GENT GOES, KURMOS SITS IN FRONT OF ROC, HIS BACK TO THE AUDIENCE. A STRONG LIGHT SURROUNDS HIM. ROC STUDIES HIM. THEIR CONVERSATION IS MOSTLY SOUND OVER)

KURMOS (recorded) Hallo.

(HE DANCES ROUND THE TREE OF LIFE.)

ROC (recorded) Surely, some little boy, made up, for 'The Dream'.

(KURMOS STOPS, STARTLED, AND STARING.)

KURMOS Can you see me? (ROC NODS.) Humans can't SEE US.

ROC Oh?

KURMOS What am I like?

ROC Two shaggy legs, two little horns, pointed chin and ears....

(KURMOS DANCES IN SMALL CIRCLES.)

KURMOS What am I doing?
ROC Dancing in small circles. (HE SITS)
KURMOS (stopping still) You must be seeing me.

(HE DANCES OVER TO ROC AND SITS BESIDE ROC.)

Why are human beings so stupid?

ROC (aloud) In what way?
KURMOS (still sound over) Such strange coverings. Some can be taken off. Why not go about in your natural state, like we do?
ROC (aloud) Clothes, we call them. For warmth and protection.
KURMOS Like you go dashing about in boxes on wheels? Sometimes bumping into each other. Is it a game?

(WITHOUT WAITING FOR A REPLY, KURMOS SKIPS ROUND THE TREE OF LIFE, REAPPEARING WITH A LOOK OF ELFIN PRIDE.)

I help trees to grow. Like this one. And that pine. Oh, all over. Only stupid humans think they can grow a tree without any help from us.
ROC Some people DO believe in nature spirits.

(KURMOS SITS BY ROC. A LONG, COMPANIONABLE SILENCE. THEN, THE BELL FOR CLOSING.)

ROC (aloud, rising) I must go...

(KURMOS NOW TALKS ALOUD)

KURMOS (unrecorded) Next time, call and I will come....
ROC Could you visit me?

KURMOS — Yes, if you invite me.

ROC — I do. I shall be delighted if you come.

KURMOS — You do believe in me?

ROC — Yes, of course I do. I have much affection for the nature spirits.

KURMOS — (leaping up) Then I'll come now...

(AGAIN, THE BELL. ROC AND KURMOS START TO LEAVE TOGETHER AS THE CITY GENT, IN A RUSH, RETURNS.)

CITY GENT — (to Roc) Good night!

ROC — (over-ordinary) Good night to you!

(KURMOS IMITATES THE GENT'S WALK FOR A MOMENT THEN, GIGGLING, PRANCES AWAY DOWN THE PATH, LEAVING ROC TO FOLLOW WITH SOME DIGNITY, IN HIS OWN TIME. AS HE GOES, ROC FADES INTO THE LESS FAY CHARACTERISTICS OF LAWSON. THIS IS TIMED SO THAT THE AUDIENCE DO NOT YET RISE FROM THEIR STOOLS.)

LAWSON — On the streets of Edinburgh, going home, Roc was amused to think what sensations might have been caused if this strange, delightful little faun had been by passers-by...! It's not just drunks that they lock up!

Reference was just made by Pan to the Greek philosophers. My own most vivid human lifetime was as a Greek scholar, a pupil of Plato. As a Greek, I saw no distinction between animate (POINTING) - that squirrel, quick as an elf - and Inanimate (pointing) - that Tree of Life. Or between spirit and matter.

In fact, we'd no separate word for matter, since we experienced spirit in ALL. That word again! This spirit could be said to sleep in the stones, dream in the plants, wake in the animals and in men, to make images, to recognise its own creation.
In my Greek life as Haemon, with the help of Plato and Pythagoras, we imagined god as a host of Olympian deities, who ruled all the worlds. This whole pantheon we kept alive by our belief. Today the cosmic interconnectedness of things and events seems to be a fundamental feature of atomic reality. Quantum theory suggests a basic oneness of the universe. This kinship of creation takes us back to where we started. Matter and energy are the same thing because indestructible spirit is in everything. Spirit is all, all is spirit.
As Greeks, we worshipped all the gods in the Pantheon. Some called us heathens. Some Pantheists.
When Pan first became visible to Roc, he thought he was seeing Kurmos again, but this time, a grown-up Kurmos. In fact, the little faun and Roc met several more times before Roc was allowed to meet the great god for real.

(RECORDED TRAFFIC NOISES ARE HEARD.)

Roc was walking home, down the Mound, late at night. Having admired the floodlit architecture of this 'Athens of the North', Roc strolled down Princes Street and turned onto the street which runs alongside the National Gallery. He was in a state of heightened awareness, as though walking naked through electrically charged cobwebs. Expectation simmered in the air.

This also happened in Iona, and at every subsequent meeting between Roc and this mighty god. And Pan always seemed to hark on FEAR.

(FROM BEHIND THE AUDIENCE, A DEEP ROUGH VOICE.)

PAN (sound over) I AM THE SERVANT OF ALMIGHTY GOD....

(THE AUDIENCE WILL TURN TO WHERE THE VOICE IS HEARD. AT FIRST, THEY WILL SEE NOTHING EXCEPTIONAL. THEN, WHAT LOOKS LIKE MOSS AND BOULDERS HIGH ABOVE THEM, BEHIND IN THE ROCK GARDEN STARTS TO MOVE. SLOWLY A MONK IS SEEN TO RISE INTO SIGHT, INTONING.)

PAN I and my subjects are willing to come to the aid of mankind, in spite of the way he has treated us and abused nature....

(HE RAISES HIS ARMS HIGH)

PAN If he affirms belief in us and asks for our help....

(THROUGHOUT THE FOLLOWING, THE VOICE OF PAN KEEPS SWITCHING BETWEEN THE MONK AND THE TREE OF LIFE. MEANWHILE, THE ROBED FIGURE DESCENDS TOWARDS THE PEOPLE. THE AUDIENCE SHOULD HAVE THEIR ATTENTION TORN BETWEEN THE MONK AND THE TREE. ROC HOLDS HIS GROUND.)

Are you afraid of me?

ROC — No.

PAN — (tree sound over) Why not? All human beings are afraid of me?

ROC — (watching the 'monk') I feel no evil in your presence. I see no reason why you should want to harm me. I'm not afraid.

PAN — (as monk) Do you know who I am?

ROC — You are the great god Pan.

PAN — (as tree) Then you ought to be afraid. Panic!

(THIS WORD 'PANIC' REVERBERATES, AS IT GETS REPEATED FROM BUSH TO BUSH, AS IF BY THE WHOLE VEGETABLE KINGDOM. 'PANIC' SURROUNDS THE ACTING AREA AND AUDIENCE WITH SURGES OF EERIE, URGENT WHISPERS.)

That word comes from the fear my presence causes.

ROC — Not always. I am not afraid. I feel an affinity with earth spirits and woodland creatures.

PAN — (monk) Do you love my subjects?

ROC — Yes.

PAN — (tree) In that case, do you love me?

ROC — Why not?

PAN — (monk, still advancing) Do you love ME?

ROC — Yes.

PAN — (monk) You know, of course, that I'm the devil? You have just said that you love the devil.

ROC — There is no evil in you. You are Pan.

PAN — (monk) Did the early Christian Church not take me as a model for the devil ...? (HE DISAPPEARS)

(THE NEXT MOMENT, PAN REAPPEARS FROM BEHIND THE TREE OF LIFE. HE IS MOSTLY HIDDEN TO THE AUDIENCE BY THE MONK'S HABIT AND COWL.)

PAN (at tree, speaking aloud) Look at my cloven hooves, my shaggy legs and the horns on my forehead. Can't you see? The Church turned all pagan gods and spirits into devils, fiends and imps.

ROC Was the Church wrong, then?

PAN The ancient gods are not necessarily devils. (HE VANISHES)

(ALMOST AT THE SAME MOMENT PAN, WITHOUT MONK'S ATTIRE, APPEARS AT ROC'S SIDE.)

PAN (with horns and hooves) What do I smell like. A goat?

(AGAIN, A SWITCH IS MADE. HAVING JUMPED, ROC TURNS TO FACE NOTHING AS, AT HIS OTHER SIDE, PAN IN MONK'S DRESS REAPPEARS.)

PAN (as monk) A goat?

ROC (sniffing) A faint, musk-like smell, like the fur of a healthy cat. Pleasant, almost like incense.

(PAN LAUGHS)

Are you still claiming to be the devil in disguise...?

PAN (after a moment) Shall we go towards my special corner...?

(TOGETHER, THEY WALK ON. THE AUDIENCE IS ENCOURAGED TO RISE AND FOLLOW IN THEIR WAKE. ALL WALK TOWARDS THE REDWOOD TREES. WE LISTEN TO THE RECORDED VOICES OF ROC AND PAN.)

PAN (sound over) You don't mind me walking beside you?

ROC (sound over) Not in the least.

(PAN PUTS AN ARM ROUND ROC'S SHOULDER.)

PAN You don't mind if I touch you?

ROC No.

PAN You really feel no repulsion or fear?

ROC None.

PAN Excellent.

(PAN LOWERS THE COWL, SHOWING HIS FAUN-LIKE HORNS. WE HAVE STILL NOT SEEN BUT A GLIMPSE OF HIS FACE. THE TRAFFIC NOISES HAVE LONG SINCE FADED.)

ROC Where are your pipes?

PAN I do have them, you know....

(NOW WE HEAR PAN PIPES ALL AROUND, RICHER AND MORE VIBRANT THAN EVER BEFORE. THESE MELODIES LEAD THE AUDIENCE ALONG THE PATH TO THE NEXT STAGE. PAN, PLAYING INVISIBLE PIPES, LEADS ROC AND THE REST. PAN VANISHES BUT THE PIPES CONTINUE TO PLAY.)

STAGE FOUR: <u>RHODODENDRON WALK</u>

(THE AUDIENCE LINGERS NEAR A CHINESE PINE. NEAR THIS THE PATH DIVIDES EITHER SIDE OF A BED FILLED WITH RHODODENDRON BUSHES. LAWSON NOW TURNS TO THE AUDIENCE WHO ARE STILL STANDING.)

LAWSON — Roc, always attracted to the theatre, was a keen amateur actor. In fact, during the filming of Dr Finlay's Casebook, Roc often stood in for Andrew Cruickshank.

One of Roc's friends told me about an event during Roc's acting days with the amateur group known as 'Makars'. They performed in Edinburgh in a little theatre known as The Pleasance. In one of their productions, Roc played the part of a character who had to summon up the Devil.

The scene was set with bubbling cauldron and low lights. After the show, Roc was besieged with questioners. How did you get that misty image to appear asked not just fellow actors but members of the audience? Next morning, banner headlines:

ACTOR SUMMONS UP DEVIL.

(THE INTENSITY OF THE MUSIC INCREASES. STRANGE LIGHTS APPEAR THROUGH THE DENSE BUSHES. FROM ONE SIDE OF ROC, PAN APPEARS HOLDING PIPES, HE BECKONS, THEN VANISHES BACK INTO THE RHODODENDRONS.)

September 1996, Attingham Park, at a weekend course conducted by Sir George Trevelyan. Roc's next experience of Pan....

(ANOTHER GLIMPSE OF PAN AS HE BECKONS, VANISHES.

ROC STARTS TO FOLLOW BUT, AS HE DOES SO, PAN AGAIN APPEARS. HE PLACES AN ARM ROUND ROC AND GUIDES HIM INTO THE RHODODENDRONS. BOTH VANISH FROM VIEW.

INCREASE ALL AUDIO-VISUAL EFFECTS. ON SOUND OVER DISEMBODIED ON ECHO, WE HEAR THE VOICE OF ROC RELATING THE NEXT EXPERIENCE AS IT HAPPENS. SEEING NOTHING OF THIS, THE AUDIENCE IS INVITED TO IMAGINE THE ACTION.)

ROC (sound over) Now Pan is near me…he steps into me... the woods are now alive, vibrant, with myriads of beings: elementals, nymphs, dryads, fauns, elves, gnomes, fairies, too many to mention. All are welcoming ...full of rejoicing...dancing in a ring. Some are minute, like those swarming on that clump of toadstools. Some are three or four feet tall, like these beautiful elfin creatures. They all love and delight in their work. As I watch, I feel outside time and space. Everything is NOW. And at the heart of this cyclone of ecstasy, deep peace. A feeling of timeless contentment....

(ROC, SOME DISTANCE FROM THE AUDIENCE, APPEARS

FROM INSIDE THE BUSHES. HE NOW HAS SHAGGY LEGS AND CLOVEN HOOVES. HE HOLDS PAN PIPES. BIRDS SING ALL AROUND HIM. HE BECKONS FOR THE AUDIENCE TO FOLLOW HIM. WITH A NEW LIBERATION, ROC DANCES TOWARDS THE REDWOOD TREES.)

STAGE FIVE: <u>THE CLEARING</u>

(THIS NEXT SCENE TAKES PLACE IN A NATURAL CLEARING IN THE WOODLAND GARDEN, NOT FAR FROM THE LAST STAGE AND A MINUTE'S WALK FROM THE RING OF REDWOOD TREES.

AS ROC APPROACHES THE NEXT STAGE, HE IS PASSED BY TWO YOUNG LOVERS. THEY DO NOT NOTICE ANYTHING STRANGE ABOUT ROC.

FOR ALL THAT, AFFECTING A STRAINED NORMALITY, ROC SITS ON THE NEARBY BENCH - AN ORDINARY MAN ON AN ORDINARY WALK IN AN ORDINARY PARK. THE LOVERS, LOOKING FOR SOMEWHERE MORE PRIVATE, CONTINUE THEIR SEARCH.

AFTER A WHILE, THREE PLUMP GNOMES APPEAR, GAMBOLLING. THEY CHASE EACH OTHER ROUND AND ROUND THE BENCH ON WHICH ROC SITS.)

ROC (thinking, sound over) How like fat children they are....

(ALL THREE ABRUPTLY STOP, SHOCKED AT WHAT THEY OBVIOUSLY HEARD. THE FATTEST TURNS ON ROC AND GLARES. STRIDING OVER TO ROC, HE PUTS HIS HAND ON HIS HIPS AND LOOKS VERY CROSS.)

FAT GNOME I'm NOT fat.

(HE TURNS AWAY, FLOUNCES OFF WITH INJURED DIGNITY. MEANWHILE, THE GIRL GNOME POINTS AT ROC'S LEGS AND ALL THREE, BURST INTO GIGGLES, DANCE OFF.

APPARENTLY LEFT ON HIS OWN, ROC STARTS TO FEED THE BIRDS AND SQUIRRELS. FROM BEHIND THE BENCH, KURMOS APPEARS. HE SKIPS TO THE FRONT AND SITS NEXT TO ROC.)

ROC This reminds me of our first meeting when you asked my why human beings are so stupid.

KURMOS (grinning) You can't answer that question, can you?

(SADLY. ROC SHAKES HIS HEAD)

ROC No, I can't. Since I've come to see the human race through the eyes of

Beings like yourself, I sometimes wonder how you can put up with us at all.

KURMOS We find human behaviour amusing at times. Often, though they ARE
destructive, cruel and horrible. Or so it seems to us. It makes us sad. We try to understand but it isn't easy....

(HE MOVES NEARER TO ROC)

We know there are those who love nature, who love this garden and find happiness and peace amongst the flowers, bushes and trees. Who love the birds and squirrels and feed them with crumbs and nuts....

(HE MOVES NEARER, THROWS A HANDFUL OF NUTS)

No doubt they could love us if they could see us. This makes us happy and we draw nearer to them....

(HE MOVES EVEN NEARER)

Some of them may even be aware of us, though they cannot see us ....

(GRINNING, HE POINTS AT ROC'S HAIRY LEGS)

KURMOS (cont'd) Why can YOU see us so clearly?

ROC' I suppose I am a privileged person. One of those chosen to link with Pan and to renew the old contact.

(SUDDENLY, PAN APPEARS.)

PAN (to Roc) Your entire life has been a preparation for this. As soon as the integration between your lower self (he points to Roc's hairy legs) and higher is achieved by a certain degree of completion, you were bound to see us. You had to be trained for more years than even a skilful brain surgeon. And that's speaking of only this one lifetime.

KURMOS (rising) Now I see!

(PAN PLACES A HAND ON THE FAUN'S HEAD)

PAN You, too, were chosen in bringing about our meeting, my little henchman.

(KURMOS LETS OUT A CRY OF JOY
THEN, WITH A BEATIFIC SMILE,
HE SKIPS OFF.)

ROC Now that I'm accepting what is happening is real, I'm getting used to the problems....

(AS IF TO PROVE HIM WRONG,
THE YOUNG LOVERS RETURN.
COVERED WITH HAIR AND CONFUSION,
ROC WRIGGLES IN THE BENCH,
ONE LEG OVER THE OTHER,
THEN THE OTHER WAY ROUND.
THOUGH BOTH THE YOUNGSTERS SEE
ROC, NEITHER NOTICES ANYTHING
ODD.

PAN, TOO, REMAINS UNNOTICED. ROC
WAITS TILL THEY'RE OUT OF EARSHOT
BEFORE MAKING COMMENT.)

ROC — I feel like Bottom with his ass's head, but the wrong way round! (pause) There was a time when I doubted. That the whole thing might be a fantasy, my unconscious. But to think of YOU as a projection, as a 'secondary personality' as the clever psychologists might maintain, seems to me totally ridiculous.

PAN — Are you sure?

ROC — Yes. A great being like yourself could never by part of my unconscious.

(PAN SMILES, CURIOUSLY.)

PAN — Have you never felt that I was within you?

ROC — Oh, yes. You've even walked into me. At Attingham. I saw the outside world through your eyes.

PAN — Would you say I possessed you?

ROC — No. It wasn't unpleasant or evil. More like identification. Integration.

PAN — Apart from those times when you have never felt I was within you.

ROC — Now, I see. We're told to seek God within us, not in just our physical body which would limit it, but in all dimensions of space and time. In the infinite, the eternal NOW. We turn away from the outside, the material world, which so many believe to be the only reality, to seek the True Reality which is within and yet, is everywhere. The whole universe is within me. The elemental kingdom, the angelic hierarchy, Christ, God Himself. This within-ness is the ALL. If we believe this, it is possible we find within what we seek. At least, a facet of the ultimate truth.

(PAN PLACES HIS HAND ON ROC'S ARM.)

PAN — I am within you, but the projection is unnecessary. To turn within is the right way. To centre oneself on the Cosmic Christ is to develop cosmic consciousness and bring about integration between the lower and the higher selves. When a certain degree of this development has been reached and you turn without, to the contemplation of the material world through the medium of the physical senses, you see it in a different way, because you are now aware of, and in touch with, the true reality behind it. Because of the ray you are on and the work you have to do, you see me and my subjects as if we were part of the material world.

This is not projection.

It is bringing cosmic reality into manifestation when it is right to do so. Of course, you do not see us as part of the material world all the time. That would be too much. Your body could not take it. It would lead to confusion. Only on rare occasion, like when you say I stepped into you, do you see the whole elemental kingdom. Or, at least, as much as you can take....

(PAN TWINKLES. THE CITY GENT APPEARS. SEEING ROC, HE HOVERS, HOPING TO TALK. HE IS UNAWARE OF PAN'S PRESENCE.)

ROC (sound over) — Can ANYONE make such a contact?

PAN (sound over) — Yes. Anyone. And it is important that this should be understood. The one-way contact is always there but being aware of the response usually needs training. Or, at least, practice. It is very subtle and easily missed.

ROC — What saddens me is when others are envious of the gifts I've been given. Why not them?

GENT (to Roc) How can I set about gaining similar experiences to your own?

(ROC HESITATES)

PAN (sound over) And you hedge!

ROC (to Gent) Some day you probably will if your faith is strong enough. Don't try too hard. It will just happen at the unexpected moment. (Sound over, to Pan) No doubt you've heard me at it!

PAN (sound over) I certainly have and it is sound advice.

ROC (to Gent) Follow my example. Live in comparative isolation in the country for ten years by yourself.

(THE GENT LOOKS AGHAST)

GENT Haven't the time. Might mean giving up too much....

(SHAKING HIS HEAD,
THE CITY GENT HURRIES OFF)

PAN (aloud, scornfully) How to see fairies in six simple lessons! There must always be time for the important things. Communicating with my subjects is not a garden game for the odd half hour. It is of vital importance for the survival of mankind. Unless man comes to realise the dangerous stupidity of outraging nature and stops the ever-increasing rate of pollution, he will ultimately destroy himself.

Seeking cooperation between the three kingdoms - the devic, the nature and man's - as is the aim of Findhorn, is one way of helping man to survive. In your case, if you had not spent those years in Cowford Cottage, you would not have seen either me, or any of my subjects.

Curiosity, it is important when its the right sort, such as seeking after truth. There is another kind. Idle curiosity. Just wanting to probe. (Ironically) "How nice it would be to be able to see lots and lots of harmless little fairies and dear little gnomes prancing about in the garden. Of course, they have very little power, but they are such fun. Little pets that don't need any looking after...."

(PAN IS NOW SWELLING WITH FIERCE POWER)

I have observed far too much of this contemptuous, superior attitude of man towards my subjects. It is almost worse than disbelief. The smallest of them has more potential power than the strongest human being. It is lucky for mankind that we are infinitely tolerant and understanding and that we obey God's will. If we used a fraction of the power we have, we could wipe the whole of mankind off the face of the earth. We are not here to be the slaves of man but to collaborate with him to bring about a world of peace, cooperation and brotherly love. A world free from wars and violence. Man's disbelief in our existence does not destroy us. It can never do that. We are here and we shall always be here even if man destroys himself and his material planet. Man is losing his domination over the other kingdoms with which he shares the earth by his destructive behaviour. He must face up to the consequences of his behaviour, which he cannot escape. If he does not, the time will come when only actions will teach him the necessary lessons. By then, it may be too late.

ROC — My dear Pan, your power is terrifying. You almost blasted me out of existence.

PAN — I'm sorry. Even I sometimes get carried away by anger. (relaxing) Let's leave it at that. (Appreciable pause) The elementals, my subjects, belong to a different evolutionary stream than man. But the one-way contact is always there. The moment you think of an entity you are in immediate communication with it.

(HIGH ON DRUGS, THE YOUNG ARTIST ENTERS. HIS SKETCHBOOK HE NOW HOLDS LIKE A SHIELD AND HIS PENCIL IS HELD OUT UNCERTAINTY, LIKE A SPEAR ABOUT TO PIERCE ANYTHING THAT IS TOO BEAUTIFUL. AS IN A DREAM, HE SEARCHES THE BUSHES. AS SOON AS HE APPEARS, THE MANNER OF THE OTHER TWO CHANGES AND THEIR VOICES RETURN TO THE SPEAKERS, BEING PRE-RECORDED.)

(sound over) — Close contact between human beings and the elementals can be dangerous if it takes place too soon. Especially if the motives for seeking it are wrong. My subjects are strange beings, as you well know. Really close links are only necessary with those who have special work to do. But not before they've reached the right degree of cosmic consciousness.

ROC (sound over) What would happen to the person who tried to summon your subjects for the wrong motives?

(THEY BOTH STUDY THE ARTIST WHO, EYES GLAZED, STARES INTO A DEEP BUSH, AS HE BREATHES IN AND OUT, NOISILY.)

PAN Such a link is easily enough made. But it would be on the wrong level. With the wrong type of being. Probably, on the lower astral plane.

ROC Tell me more about this. So far, we've been talking about the pure elementals whose basic light bodies are vortices of energy which I believe to belong to the angelic hierarchy and who take on etheric bodies formed of substances drawn from the etheric shell of the earth, in order to carry out their functions. These are the bodies that become personified as elves, fauns, fire elementals, air and water spirits, and so on. Such as are preserved in man's myths and legends.

(THE ARTIST SITS, LOTUS-FASHION.)

PAN Also goblins, the black sort; imps and others. A collection of nightmare horrors we need not go into.

ROC Those are not your subjects, then?

(PAN GIVES A LOOK OF MOCK HORROR.)

PAN Certainly not. I wouldn't acknowledge them.

ROC Do they have a god, or a leader or some sort?

PAN (Sighing) Yes, unfortunately. My opposite. Call him anti-Pan, if you like.

(THE ARTIST STARTS TO INTONE, AN ODD DISTURBING SOUND.)

ROC It sounds odd.

PAN Everything about him is odd. You might regard him as the beast aspect of myself, the detached shadow. Oh we're quite good friends, in a way, as he has a necessary part to play. I keep him at arm's' length.

ROC Is he at all like you?

PAN Well yes, in a debased sort of a way. His horns are longer and vicious looking. He has real goat's' legs and coarse hair. He smells of goat. He's the real nymph-chasing satyr, the goat-god, the true model for the devil. He's very earthly. Unfortunately, too many people take him for me. This is the reason for the bad reputation I have in some quarters.

ARTIST (still in a world of his own) Only want contact...

(THE ARTIST CHANGES HIS CHANTING. THE OTHER TWO BECOME MORE PRIVATE, THEIR VOICES STILL RECORDED.)

PAN (sound over) Invoke him with the right noises and he'll be there masquerading as me.

ROC (sound over) But you can't do something about it?

PAN More than you think. But I usually leave it, unless he goes too far. The fools who invoke him deserve what's coming to them.

ROC But do they know what they're doing?

PAN Not always. But the truth comes to the surface in the end. There is too much negative energy involved. It shows. The balance is invariably upset and brings about consequences that cannot be ignored.

ROC What sort of people can invoke him?

PAN All sorts. Often beautiful people with the highest ideals, but they are earth-oriented and have some kind of negative quality about them. Not enough cosmic consciousness.

ROC Is he evil?

PAN (looking at artist) Not necessarily. That depends on how he is evoked and by whom. He's a negative entity who brings negative energies with him.

(AT THE CLIMAX OF HIS INTONING, THE ARTIST TURNS WHITE. HIS EYES BULGE AND HE CLUTCHES HANDFULS OF HAIR. SCREAMING, HE RUNS PURSUED...)

PAN He has a role to play. But that's enough. I don't like talking about my detached shadow...

(THROUGH THE BUSHES INTO WHICH THE ARTIST WAS STARING, PAN VANISHES. ROC TRIES TO FOLLOW. HE IS STOPPED BY A RUSTLE IN THE UNDERGROWTH. HE IS AWARE OF THE POWERFUL ODOUR OF PINE NEEDLES, AN ACID EARTH-LIKE SMELL. TWO FACES, WITH SHARP GREEN EYES, EMERGE FROM THE SHRUBBERY.)

1st FACE Mortal man, do not dare to come any farther. This is our territory.

ROC (startled) I'm a friend of Pan's and I'm a friend of all the Nature Beings. I come here to Rosemarkie, like a child, with love in my heart.

2nd FACE	We have no love for you, man. Go back to where you came from and leave us in peace.

(THEY EMERGE FROM THE BUSHES. TWO LITTLE PEOPLE, WITH GREEN CLOAKS AND HOODS, GREEN SKIN. THEY HOLD GREEN BOWS AND ARROWS, THE TIPS SHARP AND POINTING AT ROC.)

ROC	I believe in you and want your friendship and help. Look ...! (he indicates his hairy legs.)
1st ELF	This is our stronghold on the Black Isle. We want no mortals here.

(AFTER A MOMENT, THE ELVES CONFER.)

	Proceed. But that man (He points)
2nd ELF	On that stump. (To Roc) Proceed.

ROC (to invisible Peter) Such hostility. Just look at the damage done to this Fairy Glen. The fallen trees and the cut-off stumps. Man's done some terrible deeds around here, Peter, since I was young. In here must be their only refuge....

(ROC GOES INTO THE BUSHES FOLLOWED BY THE TWO ELVES. ALL THREE BECOME INVISIBLE TO THE AUDIENCE. MUSIC IS HEARD, MUTED TUNING OF STRINGS AND FLUTES. AS PHOSPHORUS LIGHTS FLICK ON AND OFF, CHANGING COLOURS, WE ALSO HEAR AN EERIE, AGGRESSIVE WHISPERING. THE WORDS ARE ALL NOW PRE-RECORDED.)

(sound over) I'm captured. These elves dart about and spit like fireworks. Their anger is like a wail of grief. Look, the leaves dancing, struggling to be free, like flags on sinking ships...

ELF KING (sound over) Man, we have no understanding of you.

ROC Yes, your majesty.

ELF KING Sit.

ROC Yes, your majesty.

(BEAUTIFUL YOUNG LOVERS, ARM IN ARM, ENTER. AS BEFORE, THEY'RE ONLY AWARE OF THEMSELVES)

ELF KING You upset the balance of nature, destroy the animals, turn the land to desert, cut and burn large trees, maim the landscape, blasting great wounds in the hills and mountains, slashing the living earth so that it will not heal.

1st ELF You pollute everything beneath you and everything above you. Everywhere you go is fouled and destroyed.

2nd ELF Are you so stupid that you cannot realise you are destroying yourself?

ELF KING You cannot destroy us, for we are immortal and indestructible. But we care about this planet, we love it, it is our home and abode. It was once beautiful. Can you blame us if we consider you a parasite on the face of the earth?

(AS THOUGH ALONE, THE LOVERS SINK DOWN ON THE GRASS.)

2nd ELF YOU!

1st ELF YOU!

ELF KING You have the effrontery to ask for our cooperation! In what? In the devastation of our strongholds? Our sacred places? Our dwellings? Justify your request! Explain yourself. What is the meaning of your life, man?

(WITHIN, A RUSTLE OF LEAVES AND ELFIN OUTRAGE.)

ROC — Mankind is not evil. The majority of the inhabitants of this Earth are peace-loving and kind and want to live in friendship with all. This is the truth ....

(SOUNDS OF DISBELIEF.)

ROC — It is easy to see bad deeds. It is less easy to see good ones. But to be fair, you must try to do so.

(A TWO-WAY FLOW OF RESPONSES WITHIN. THE LOVERS ALSO MURMUR.)

There are many people every bit as distressed as I am at the outrages committed, at the cruelty and destruction inflicted on the animal kingdom and the raping of the mineral kingdom. Your majesty, on behalf of those who are wantonly destroying the earth, I can say nothing....

(SOUNDS OF 'SHAME, SHAME. LOVERS BECOME UNEASY.)

They disbelieve in you now. But more and more are becoming to accept your existence. So it is up to us to convince you that we care. Be fair to us. Help us.

(A SILENCE. EXCEPT, THAT IS, FOR THE LOVERS, GROANING, LUXURIOUSLY.)

ELF KING We listen. We watch.
ROC Could you destroy mankind if you wanted to?
KING Easily.
ROC How?
KING The vital force in all that grows would cease.

(TOTAL SILENCE.)

ROC Would that mean the end, in accordance with God's will?
KING If Man goes too far he will destroy himself - he doesn't need us for that. He has freewill. But we cannot break cosmic laws which are God's laws.
ROC Man is turning within now. More and more people seek to understand. Everything is now changing. A new age.
KING Well, we will do nothing to hurt you. But if Man enters where he is not wanted, or acts to destroy, then do not blame us if we play TRICKS...!

(AT THIS WORD, AN EXPLOSION OF ELFIN MIRTH. ROC BURSTS OUT OF THE BUSHES. STARTLED, THE LOVERS RISE AND FLEE. ROC NO LONGER WEARS THE HAIRY LEGS.)

ROC (with growing agitation) Man has developed his intellect and lost all the other kingdoms, thus gaining greater skills in trickery, cheating, beating his fellow men. How can your subjects bear to share the earth with us? There are times when

I'm bitterly ashamed of my fellow human beings.

(PAN APPEARS, PLACES AN ARM ROUND ROC.)

PAN — You mustn't look on the black side like this. Your higher self must be off duty. I shall have to take his place. Man is also doing great and beautiful things. Many men reach great spiritual heights in their lifetime. Sometimes, they are great beings in incarnation. Concentrate on the good and the beautiful. Turn your back on the sensational headlines. Read. Listen to music, lose yourself in fine paintings.

ROC — (quietly) Of course you are right.

(FOR A MOMENT, THEY ARE QUIET.)

PAN — My seeming appearance is Greek, though my origin is much older. What do you feel when people say that I must be ugly?

ROC — Disgusted and horrified. What they are criticising is an imaginary picture, but I mustn't blame humans for their lapses. You are a being of incredible beauty.

PAN — Gross flattery will get you nowhere!

ROC — It happens to be the truth.

PAN — Unfortunately, my debased counterpart, anti-Pan, received most attention from the artists, because he is more easily contacted.

ROC — And what of the legends and ballads that tell of the misfortunes that overtake those who get involved with Fairyland? Disappearing into hollow hills for years like Rip Van Winkle?

PAN — And what of the Hobbits and the elves of Rivendale? So far, YOU have not disappeared!

ROC — (surprised) You read Tolkien?

PAN — My literary tastes are impeccable! I don't read, of course. But, in a way, I am involved. I suppose you know you're close ...(he points to the bushes) .... to the elves than to any of my other subjects. Do you feel lost?

ROC — I believe in God, my link with the Cosmic Christ is strong, I'm dedicated to work for the light... (HE SITS ON THE BENCH)

All the same, I feel in some way different....

PAN — Does it worry you?

ROC — No, it is part of the price I have to pay and I do so, willingly. (grinning) I don't have any choice, do I?

PAN — Not much.

(ROC, WITH JOY BREATHES
IN AND OUT AS HIS EYES SCAN
THE GARDEN.)

ROC — The whole vegetable kingdom ...such livingness ...even in the autumn 's... vital...timeless....

PAN — And who, do you suppose, are the artists responsible for changing the colours of these leaves around us...?

ROC — (realising) Oh, I'd never thought of that!

PAN — Of course, the Botanist will tell you differently. He doesn't believe in fairies. He has HIS explanation, I have MINE. Which do you think is right...?

(ROC HESITATES)

Take your choice.

ROC (after a moment) Both.

PAN You develop in wisdom.

ROC (looking around) I have good teachers.

(HE SALUTES THE TREES AND BUSHES)

PAN Yes, even the trees rustle in their appreciation, murmuring their gratitude.

(ROC LOOKS SURPRISED)

Indeed, they now accept you as one of their own.... listen....

(ROC CLOSES HIS EYES. HE IS DEEPLY MOVED. PAN TAKES BOTH HIS HANDS INTO HIS OWN.)

ROC I'm overwhelmed by this tremendous overflow of love. My life HAS been worthwhile, after all...

PAN We chose you. Yet you began it yourself....

ROC (surprised) How? When?

PAN (smiling) Patience.

(ROC NODS, SMILING WRYLY. THEY SHARE A SILENCE.)

All the time you lived at Cowford Cottage you were unaware of the Nature Spirits,
In spite of your lifelong interest in esoteric and occult subjects.

ROC At that time I'd have dismissed belief fairies, gnomes or elves as superstition. As figments.

PAN The results of your scientific training?

ROC I tried to find rational explanations for the psychic manifestations that I'd studied but there were certain phenomena I had to accept. I could NOT explain away. And perhaps it's possible that molecules such as DNA have an etheric counterpart. While it's true that man can modify nature's handiwork, it became clear that, instead of using force to do so, he would be better to ask the Nature Spirits first. Let THEM modify the etheric counterparts. For already they are withdrawing from plants, farms and gardens.

PAN Why did you ask for my help at Findhorn?

ROC The soil was sandy, originally covered by only gorse, broom and scrub pine.

PAN You wanted it to yield beautiful trees, shrubs and flowers?

ROC And vegetables, yes.

PAN And did it?

ROC The chestnut tree averaged 14 inches, despite the first summer being dry. But why are you asking these questions? You must be able to read my mind. The past. The Future. So you already know the answers.

PAN In reviewing your memories, the most vital years of your life, you will see how the bridges were built between your exoteric and esoteric ideas and experiences, and the way they've been integrated. By studying how this was brought about in your own case, you may be able to help others to build their bridges.

ROC I see. (RISING) As a boy, I loved the Greek myths, yet if anyone had suggested that I might one day see and talk to and even touch one of them, I would have started laughing and said, UTTER RUBBISH! Instead, I developed an obsessional interest in physics and chemistry.

PAN What was I to you, then? Was I the evil spirit who produced panic in woods, a devil?

ROC No. You were Pan as in 'The Wind in the Willows' ....

(PAUSE. HE SEEMS TO FIND A NEW THOUGHT.)

Surely, you've ALWAYS been the wonderful and beautiful being you are to me now...

PAN This is the reason you were not afraid of me when I appeared. One of the reasons you were chosen. In you I found a mediator between our worlds. Try to lift the stigma that was imposed on me by the early Church.

(THEY START TO WALK AWAY, TOGETHER.)

ROC The coming years will show to what extent this is happening....

(STRANGERS APPEAR AND PASS, NOTICING NOTHING STRANGE.)

ROC To me you are so real. More real than the people around who cannot see you....

PAN Of course I am more real, the true reality rejected by most....

(PAN TAKES OUT HIS PIPES. KURMOS APPEARS. PLUS THE ELVES SEEN EARLIER. THEY ALL SING AS PAN PLAYS. THE AUDIENCE IS LED ALONG THE PATH.)

ALL (singing)

HE IS GREAT AND HE IS JUST
HE IS GOOD, AND MUST
THUS BE HONOURED, DAFFODILLIES;

(PAN VANISHES BUT THE PIPES CONTINUE. IN THE SIMPLER PARTS OF THE SONG, THE AUDIENCE, THE WORDS IN THEIR PROGRAMME, MAY BE ENCOURAGED TO JOIN IN, SINGING WITH THE ACTORS.)

ROSES, PINKS AND LOVED LILIES,
LET US FLING WHILST WE SING
EVER HOLY, EVER HOLY,
EVER HONOURED! EVERY YOUNG,
THE GREAT GOD PAN IS EVER SUNG.

(DURING THIS SINGING, ROC HAS LED ALL, ACTORS AND AUDIENCE OUT OF THE WOODLAND GARDEN. KURMOS KEEPS DARTING IN AND OUT, TRYING TO GET AND HOLD THE ATTENTION OF ROC. AT THE BOTTOM OF THE SLOPE, THEY ALL RIGHT WHEEL AND COME TO REST.)

STAGE SIX: <u>THE CROSS ROADS</u>

(AT LAST, KURMOS BLOCKS ROC'S PROGRESS WITH AN EXAGGERATED BOW. ALL COME TO REST AT THE BOTTOM OF THE SLOPE KNOWN AS THE GLADE. THERE, THE AUDIENCE WILL STAND ON THE NORTH SIDE OF THE PATH, UNDER THE ASH TREE (L87567).

THEY WILL BE FACING TOWARDS THE EAST, GRASS ON THEIR RIGHT. THREE PATHS ARE IN FRONT OF THEM. ALSO A SIGNPOST. THE AUDIENCE STANDS.)

KURMOS (to Roc, bowing) In exalted company today. Am I welcome?

ROC You are always welcome.

KURMOS Are you going back to the flat?

ROC Come along. You'll be very welcome. (HE GESTURES TOWARDS THE WEST GATE.)

KURMOS Part of the way. This is one of my busy days.

ROC Is it?

KURMOS Yes. (with a laugh) I'm glad I was the first Nature Spirit you saw.

ROC Are you becoming conceited about it?

KURMOS What is conceited?

ROC Being pleased with yourself and showing it.

KURMOS (laughing) I'm always pleased with myself. Is that wrong?

ROC No. In your case, you have every right to be.

KURMOS Aren't you pleased with yourself?

ROC Not very often.

KURMOS But you ought to be. Existence is so joyful.

ROC Only rarely so for human beings.

KURMOS (sadly) I know that's true from the things I see.

ROC This garden helps, Kurmos. But I fail in so many things.

KURMOS Not with Pan and with us. Isn't that something to be pleased about?

ROC I'm privileged, yes I know.

KURMOS That's better. You know we all love you and will help you as much as we can. All of us.

ROC — Thank you. Now I must go. It's your busy day.

KURMOS — (chuckling) It's my busy day....

(HE DARTS OFF THROUGH THE TREES, THEN DASHES ACROSS THE LAKE WITH HARDLY A SPLASH. FOR THE LAST TIME, ROC IS REPLACED BY LAWSON.)

LAWSON — The first time Kurmos visited Roc's flat (he gestures towards the West Gate) the little faun expressed great interest in the large collection of books. But then he added, somewhat enigmatically, that one can get all the knowledge one wants. How? By simply wanting it, ENOUGH.

Are we back again to making thought-forms, moulds? Back, in short, to WISHING; wishing in a Holy Well, perhaps. Well third time lucky, they say. And here we are at a crossroads, with three choices. Three routes out of the garden:

(HE POINTS TO THE FIRST TWO BRANCHES OF THE SIGNPOST, READING ALOUD THE WORDS:)

The "WEST GATE". Heavy with materialism. The "EAST GATE". Heavy with mysticism. Or...the Un-named.

(THE THIRD BRANCH OF THE SIGNPOST IS BLANK.)

LAWSON — On the road to the Oracle in Delphi, to be seen about 30 miles outside Athens, there is the crossroads where Oedipus killed his father. This fork is symbolic of the three roads where soul meets the lower selves and slays them. That would leave the middle path, the Unnameable. Well, maybe it leads to Pan's Special Corner, as Roc called it. The wild part that every garden ought to preserve in its natural state, undisturbed for the elementals to make their home.

LAWSON Or, maybe, the middle path leads to the realms above the psychic, worlds of pure spirit, above the pain of all alternatives. The balance between the positive and the negative, the masculine and the feminine. The well-adjusted middle way, neither being for, nor against. At least, all roads lead to home, on one level or another.

"Proceed in faith". This is what Pan says in his last conversation with Roc. Often, back in his flat late at night, Roc would be struggling to get the facts of their talks together absolutely correct. Shall we proceed in faith...?

(HELEADS THE AUDIENCE THE MIDDLE WAY, LED BY THE BLANK SIGNPOST. THIS PATH LEADS BACK TO TJE ROCK GARDEN. THE AUDIENCE THIS TIME LOOKS AT THE WATERFALL FROM BELOW. FIRST, THEY TURN WHLE STANDING ON THE PATH. ROC IS WRITING.)

STAGE SEVEN: ROCK GARDEN PATH

(ON THE LAWN NORTH OF THIS PATH ARE PLACED TWO ARMCHAIRS. BY ONE, THERE IS A WRITING-TABLE. ON THIS A NOTEBOOK, PEN AND INK.)

ASSUMING THE PART OF ROC, THE ACTOR STARTS TO WRITE. THEN HE HESITATES, HIS FACE FULL OF DOUBTS.)

ROC — Did all these exchanges actually take place the other day or are you giving me more while I'm writing? Or am I adding anything myself? It's important to me that it's authentic.

(IN THE OTHER ARMCHAIR, PAN APPEARS.)

PAN — In your own Higher Being, you know that it is. Our conversations take place in the form of images and symbols. Some are not fully realised into words by your mind at the time. But they were deeply impressed into your unconscious level and are now being realised into words under my guidance. I am over-lighting you during the whole of this transcript. Nothing is being left out. Nothing added. Personal colouration on your part is kept down to a minimum. I will give you any corrections. Proceed in faith.

ROC — Thank you for the reassurance.

PAN — Now I want to return to your life at Cowford Cottage. I want you to realise its full significance.

ROC — What am I not realising?

PAN — At the time you knew nothing about Power Points and their associated ley lines.

ROC — That's true.

PAN — Doesn't it surprise you to learn there was a powerful Nature Point behind the outhouses?

ROC — In the middle of the wood?

PAN (twinkling) — Yes. The exact spot you used to sunbathe on.

ROC (startled) — Oh no, this is fantastic!

PAN	All through those ten years ... you lay naked on a PowerPoint.
ROC	On a waterproof sheet....
PAN	Rubber does not insulate you from those energies.
ROC	I felt nothing. I thought the energy was coming from the sun.
PAN	You were not so sensitive in those days. You were lying in the air, lying on the earth, in the sun'S rays. Afterwards, you bathed in the stream.
ROC	Yes, I'd damned it to make a pool.
PAN	The sun symbolises the fire so, in all, you had close frequent contact with the four elements over a long period. At that power point, for over ten years, all your bodies were being prepared. Not only that. It was a place associated with pre-Christian ceremonies and rituals of a Druidic nature. Also, it was a hillock.
ROC	At the time, all I knew was.... is that it was the right place for me.
PAN	It certainly was. That is all. For the moment.

(PAUSE. ROC CLOSES HIS NOTEBOOK.)

ROC	I suppose knowledge gained at a later date is not always carried back...' ....

(CHILDREN ARE HEARD, SHOUTING.)

...carried back to an earlier time....

(THE CHILDREN ARE THE ONES SEEN EARLIER, TWO BOYS AND A GIRL. THE YOUNGEST REPRESENTS ROC.

THE AUDIENCE WILL NOW TURN TO FACE THE ROCK GARDEN.)

ROC — (child) I'm not tellin' anybody. Secret.

GIRL — Be fair, Robert. Just tell ME.

(THE YOUNG ROC SHAKES HIS HEAD.)

BOY — Then Liz an' me, we won't play with you. See how you like THAT...!

(THEY LEAVE ROC ALONE. AFTER A MOMENT, THE BOY TAKES A PENNY FROM HIS POCKET AND SINGS:)

ROC — (the boy, singing)

O WISHING WELL, WISHING WELL
MY WISH BE HEARD.
WHEN I WAS A FISH,
I LONGED TO BE A BIRD.

ONE, TWO, THREE
SING A LITTLE SPELL,

ROC — DROP YOUR PENNY
IN THE WELL. (Roc does so)
MAKE A WISH AND MAKE IT BOLD
LET ME SEE (he closes his eyes, holds his nose)
LITTLE FAIRIES UNFOLD!

(HE OPENS HIS EYES. FROM BEHIND THE BOULDERS ABOVE, THE TWO OTHER CHILDREN SUDDENLY REAPPEAR, JEERING.)

BOTH KIDS — Fairies, fairies, Robbie believes in fairies...!

YOUNG ROC — Don't ....don't....don't...I DON'T!

OLD ROC I DON'T, I DON'T!

(PAN PIPES ARE HEARD, THE BOY IS CRYING.)

And I didn't. Not again for over SIXTY YEARS!

(HE PICKS UP HIS YOUNGER SELF AND PERCHES HIM ON HIS SHOULDERS.)

OLD ROC (cont'd) Even long forgotten wishes can come true. Proceed in faith...

(YOUNG AND OLD ROC TOGETHER MOUNT THE STEPPINGSTONES UP STREAM UNTIL THEY VANISH OVER THE BROW OF THE ROCK GARDENS. MUSIC. LIGHTS FADE.

TIME TO GO HOME – THANK YOU ALL!

LIFE WHISPERER?

Past mating duels and past conflicts now done. Wisdom
again begun. All players preparing every encore
Outer silence reunited in a single note until evermore First
Word - the sound of love. All outside was once simmering
within.
Cosmic orchestra gives life till harmonies end strife
Each instrumentalist's unique score.

A BOMB BOOM-ERANG?

BIGGEST world Wind Farm in Cumbria. Plus, Sellafield's
nuclear reprocessing plant, 1/15 operational reactors in
UK's tiny island.
Globally, 10 serious accidents
So far. Forget fires and radioactive leaks
Let alone Japan's Hiroshima? Choking unseen garden
gnome
As nuclear waste travels around Britain
Seeking a permanent (sic) home?
(See author's 20 imperfect peace poems,
THE MUSHROOM MEN*)*

SEED-SORES?

Thin green shame mankind slowly swaying from side-to-side
Seeking a safe place from the truth to hide
There to thrive and feed
To flourish and breed. Fulfilling all potential healthy resources
As essential for Future's healthy survival of broods
All adapting to weather's moods.

Seeding rainclouds or poisoning trusting crowds?

FATALITIES?

Decarbonisation decide, less global warming deride,
Hot air overheats, profit pundit cheats.
Let earth be loved where we abide.
9000,500 dying from air pollution in London yearly.
Since 2010, suicide statistics risen,
Including schoolchildren reaching 14-year high, mostly males.
Their personal exam stress abuse makes
As State's learning regime pales.

THE FLOODED DUTCHMAN

Low- lands beware. Dutchmen aware of sea levels,
the Netherlands sinking as UK tilts
Somewhat protected by sand-dunes and dykes.
What continent on floods not verging
Waters fresh and salty soon merging?
Regimented hybrid bisexual tulips on a plinth,
Trade rivalled by sweetly scented hyacinth.
Emblematic flowers/animals statistics
Describe national characteristics?

CARRY ON FLIRT

Not dumb, every creature communicates
As each to environment relates
Male feeding her a tasty morsel
Hen harrier's upside-down as she mates. Aerobatics they
together try some out-skilling the dragonfly.
Crested grebes dance before they fornicate,
Imitating shared movements till they mate.
Thus many wild ones over-breed, premature death often
their fate.

TITCHWELL NATURE RESERVE

Tree felled for past sea-defences logs in marshes,
From the Crown Estate land rented.

Salted freshwater pools, by salmon unscented.

Coastal foreshores grow sandwort, hornwrack, lavender,
pink sea aster glasswort, often covering sunken forests of
oak, elm and elder
Remnants revealed as each tide passes.
Sand-dunes anchored by deep-rooted grasses.

MOUNTAIN TEMPLES - 1 -

Quartz crystals on Peru's horse-killer tracks
Tempting climbers' to reach unconquered granite peaks.
22 for seconds' drop dead below to die.
Rain-bulged clouds in the sky.
Reward; breathless views for dazzling eyes
10 hours later Nature's amazing hazards include high

Snow-caps
Magnanimously melting
13 miles smoking magna
Chambers rocks smelting.

MOUNTAIN TEMPLES - 2 -

Andes, the youngest mountain ranges.
Man earth's vistas rearranges,
Mountains overruling men shaping
Graceful wind-sculpted blue-white dunes,
Snow still sticking to cliff faces.
Soon fridge-cold floods swamp rivers lakes and lagoons.
Power-mad mankind with harpoons
Disgraces digested for fine shares invested.
Too many criminal acts knighted. Honoured but not
indicted?

MOUNTAIN TEMPLES - 3 -

Too high…too cold…too airless for most creatures
5,200 meters above rooks and foothills' leeches.
Feather-cloaked finches in ice nooks on inches
Twigs as nest, from zero degrees a rest.
On perilous edge brief timescale to fledge
Threatened by sun-sparked avalanches
Sweeping nest downwards leaves no branches…sticks…
Or chicks' ranches.

MOUNTAIN TEMPLES - 4 -

Hidden valleys in the Himalayas hide holy Adepts who've
outgrown prayers. Yak tea and ether sustaining beyond
complaining,
Higher than eagles' birds'-eye vision
Unperturbed as non-ailing old teach physical revision.
Within dreams and secret discourse
Mystic Masters work with love, not force.
Total independence decided.
Support for the ascendant guided.

RENEWABLE POWERS

Biscuits and mince pies without palm oil more general
Albino orangutan its friendless central
Unlike over-angry conservationist
Judged dangerous as to others a Creationist
Fossil fuels overtaken by plants undercover
Not yet sterilised as being weeds un-needed
Insects' ancestors bred in the wild
Weedy herbs in wildernesses now less reviled?

MORNING GLORIES

128X44 in 2018 for botanists never too late
And maybe never will be so
Finding safe flora every year before they go.
Aquatic plants further dull horizons will brighten
Foul air, reducing for clean skies to heighten
Magic fungi species now number 44
Watercress illuminating streetlamps more
Optimism's ever-open door.

RESURGENCY

Our originating Void never empty watery womb filled with plenty
Self-consuming eagle ego claws out its own entrails
Yet matter's metamorphism never fails
Mother Nature by humanity crushed
As corks in water need not be rushed
Resurfacing from spaces unseen
Reshaping itself new flushed, no green growth an eternal has-bean.

UNIFYING MELODIES

'When and why did birds learn to sing?
Ann ask, how did plovers get their ring,
Butterflies their bling, or nettles their sting,
Or buttercups become a king,
And bluebells their ting-a-ling
As wasps will sting
Anything
As late summer seedpods open spring
Jaguars get their mating zing.
Only consciousness can advantages bring!

DISAPPEARING

Different characters all creatures,
Varied experiences life's teachers
From gaggle gander to loner panda
All earth's characters outgrow preachers.
Evolution we all help progress,
With culling pruning, Life not repressed
With new incorrigible growth sun-caressed?
Death is no deterrent the wise will confess
Love's tough Laws eventually ways bless.

GONE FOR EVER?

Large throbbing red blob will swallow earth.
Gaia killed might believe in rebirth as did Lemuria and Atlantis
Till Seabed Mountains surfacing rearose after repose?
Atoms transmute and evolve every yo-yo spiral will revolve.
Like Jupiter's waters rattle scientists as climates unsettle
Yet in certain conditions some gasses become metal.

ADAPTIONS

As yak migrate later, Artic Inuits under iced-covered sea
At low tides through pick-pierced holes,
Women harvest muscles in white plastic buckets.
Elsewhere environmentalists handled
Discarded fishing equipment, 30 tonnes of coastal plastic tangled
Poachers for world health's sexy markets' till.
Stalking ivory tusks. Still valuable elephants and rhinos kill.

ZONES - 1 -

Burnt-out bullets wayward thumbs lie where no bee hums
Verdant battlefields battered bloomless waste.
Unexploded testicles, bloodless legs empty boots laced
Eyeless gasmasks, disembowelled tanks.
Sweethearts' letters utter thanks.
Faceless lovers mutter déjà vu...
Pleas repeated breathlessly, "See you..." Alive later seeking archives
Who'll see sepia soldiers through renewed eyes?

ZONES - 2 -

Bulletproof vests not for bang-bang but tweet-tweet.
Reclaiming marshlands Destroyed local wildlife in retreat.
Dammed river re-released overflows for new reed-beds' beasts.
Attractions, warblers and fish. Tomorrow's peaceful tourists' wish
Political upheavals pacified new-born creatures poachers now breeding their family on part-time immigrant flocks feeding
Feathered friends cluck but don't...
Duck!

WISH BONES

Basic building-blocks with malleable flesh-dressed bones
Versatile Nature breeds birds, ants and beehives' drones.
Dragonflies outsmarting helicopters don't crash
Optimistic infinity love's wishes never dash.
Shortage of feed animals don't breed
Shrewdest diagnosis adopts symbiosis
And interdependence
Pressures on temperatures In the Azores
Global Warming's dangers could curb Cold Wars?

PILAGING

Sea-lice eat Salmon. Bulging milky sludge farms breed fat fish
For fishmongers appeal fish a fine meal
For quick-fix suppers - Plastic cutlery wildlife scuppers
Illegal as landfilling, thriving humans do harm by overkilling
Grouse for gourmets' grilling
Fly-tipped bin-bags burst by sea-gulls' beaks
As Keep Britain Tidy worker, unheard, shrieks.

LOOPY

Save planet earth possible now,
Boulders giving information how
Glaciers behaved by Nature engraved
No tree any one leaf returns to bough
Individuality divinity broadly will endow
Mankind broadcasting vanity's self-seeking row
With warring cries all tragedies surprise
Same mistakes on circular tours of Causes' effects
Wisdom's whispers ego.

APING

Monkeys at water stations share with thirsty relations
Plastic beakers, none incontinent leakers
Imbibing through plastic straws playing Poohsticks
Till nearby seashores become non-biodegradable graves
Bathing unavailable as plastic waves
Fifty miles from nearest isle bash into its bulging plastic bile
Consuming seas' corpses, The Hundredth Monkey
which law enforces?

NOW YOU SEE US, NOW...

As peppered month to factory's trees clung
Bird beaks after nipping them when still young
Black soot-coated trunks not safe to roost
To give new young their survival chances to boost
Though death can never defeat the Life Force
Creative consciousness too clever, of course,
No lame duck gets goosed.

EMPATHY

Transliterate whales' speech melancholy about
Dominant mankind's damaging developments
As moths adapting to Industrial Revolution suggested evolution
Never permanently arrested, Natural Order staying in charge.
Geese weather-predictors, Lorenz whispered to their eggs.
Sentimental? Elemental?
Humanising animals seeing star-types, calling them by names.
Man's best friend rescue injured owners playing games.

WASTE OF SPACE

2000 tonnes of junk in space
Seas choke as litter grows apace
Car fumes cause Alzheimer's disconnections.
Gone global goodwill and grace?
Meanwhile, oceans plump with plastic waste
Ambitious escapees to other planets race.
Astronaut repairing craft his screwdriver let go
Maybe laughed.
It will live longer than men below?

ASSOCIATED SOILS

Different soils suit certain plants not others.
Some respond as if they're enemies, not brothers
Now man's planted species grow on alien lands
Often occupied by foreign hands with different dietary tastes
Maybe discarding healthy wastes
Judged obnoxious trash indulgent beings too rash.
Earths needs renewal as fires need fuel.

MOODS

Ann feels unworthy sometimes sort of rotten.
Early Self-esteem forgotten. Her Grandad helps, when agony yelps.
Walking in woods under green boughs, there to renew stale vows
Smelling meadow flowers re-empowers.

Barefoot, tripping through dew-dappled grasses as sunbeams renew Gaining healings with country ambles
Disentangling knotted problems
Like spiky brambles.

MIRRORS - 1 -

City-civilised wild beasts sniff out feasts
Due to habitat depletion
For holy developers' estates' completion
Wild animals as domesticated pets gain the advantage of vets
Before becoming human bipeds
Sleeping maybe in housekeepers' beds
Cuddly cuteness their visa passes.
Ego sees similarities. Flattery in looking glasses
Greedy pets licking arses.

MIRRORS - 2 -

Urban racoons more sophisticated than their country cousins. Opportunists in the wild become downgraded
By settling in houses our homes raided
Housed raccoons more resourceful than a two-year-old child.
Human lives restyled. Creatures' play their keepers.
Not only kids are creepers.
'Lonely elephants in distress Ann will die of stress.'

FAIR COPS?

Roadside fields feeding milk and meat cows in herds and
cars by the fleet. No public transport pollution report
Politicians hide, shared profits in support. Top secret police
masked
Undercover married male bed-mates
Probing lady environmental protesters' estates
Undermining their efforts to save
Mankind's habitat and health our corporate wealth.

PEACE PATH cg

Bridal Ways Lovers' Lanes Footpaths threatened
Through every historic war peace beckoned
Trenches waterlogged, men fighting peace befogged
As shells fell grass buds wounded with craters
Squaddies Bosh haters writing love to their maters
After Armistice let one path link all war-torn fields
Following No-Man's-Land as doleful bell peace peals

BRAINS - 1 -

Manatees' body covered in whiskers helps their intelligence
Like elephants.
Raccoons see through hands not eyes,
Manatees too, scientists surprised
Despite small brains flirt with alligators
In sauna lagoons no longer predator wary,
Shared comfort zones, no enemy jaws scary.
Some bears and crows, brighter than two-year-old child
Despite being wild

BRAINS? - 2 -

Inbred curiosity…landscape fun…
Super-intelligent dolphins, dogs, apes,
Learn through play and japes.
Problem-solving brain-cells revolving, tortoise mind to
function
Needs warmth, especially when she's on heat,
Not slow then to show Mister T her female glow.
Rats' facing hidden threats foe poses, super-sensitive noses
Find TNT, explosive landmines located
Safely detonated.

RECALL

God was lonely until creating nature's range.
Different shapes some seeming strange,
Many creatures' serial killers
Stark fairytales as kids' stocking-fillers,
Pages of animals in human pickles,
Thrilling readers with emotions' prickles.
These prepared Ann for adult woes
Often revisiting problems, she already knows,
Enticed into Granddad's wise advice.

MOUNTAIN MEMOIRS

Ghostly carbon's dangers assumed unseen this manmade
cause, despite optimistic laws…revealing its flaws,
Yashmaks mask babies on all-fours
Premature geriatrics reopening deaths' doors.
Oceans deposit on shores bottled pleas for help, plastic not
draped in kelp, message recycled, long-lived like
parchment, plastic or fossils mountaintops found not
poisoning our ground.

SYCHRONICITY

Totem animals' characteristics shared. North American
Indians fared
Prey pictured before hunting; all animal parts used
Nature not abused.
Clichés like sly as foxes; obstinate as donkeys; mischievous
as monkeys, Saints being prepared as Shaman
In wild-reared skins adorned as tribal followers fawned,
Seeking free blessings plus their painful lessons.

REGRESSION

Radios need to be wireless for technology to progress
Ideally gismos without commerce-driven obsolescence.
Animals lose their livelihood…
Whether in forests, savannahs
Arctic's shrinking expanses, factory floors
Parched sunburnt palaces.
Now circus beasts free from servitude confined to zoos
Offspring astute students with special needs
Sent back to inhospitable outdated schools.

OFFACTION

Dogs beat all slugs' noses sniffing out malaria
Facts not known through Freud's hysteria.
Wallace exploring hyacinths and wisteria
Nature's evolution he and Darwin's revolution
Father of ecology and psychology
Searching jungles' saunas sweating
In separate boxes no apology
Freud explaining dreams and bed-wetting
Wallace not competing or go-getting

METAMORPHIS

Extinction cannot so put dodos on this list
And add in unicorns on the astral plane
Repeated appearances to keep scientists sane.
If dreams deemed suitable data as proof
Even awake above you can see through your roof.
Wolves dream they're Red Riding Hood
Like rebirth dismissed so-called bloodlust, misunderstood.

APPETITES

What's enough food for baby hedgehogs?
Deserted by mum a plaything for dogs
Prickles and snuffles before babe shuffles
Save endangered kit from bonfires and bogs

Tame every creature with food it adores
For pets many boys choose dinosaurs
Their fossils found in Mexico's Bay
Spring's buds rebirth
Another
Day

ETERNALLY EXTANT?

3 species daily dumped in extinction's dustbin
Evolution will eventually rust best bling
Delegating dinosaurs and unicorns to dreams

Like departed pet cats lapping up astral creams
Till their number calls, 'To earth again your wish!'
Found a coelacanth the prehistoric lobe-finned fish
Near Indonesia to awaken secular pessimists' amnesia.

REFLECTIONS

Civic trees expensive to maintain as council financial cuts remain. Beneath trees where starlings roost, cars parked under their boughs.
Motor economies chief boost, despite public's protectionist vows.
The car is king. Free enterprise.
Forget skies swept by murmurs, feathered flocks as acrobatic
As fish with fins seemingly looking aquatic

TIMELESS VEILS

See all life as fabulous confections
Reproduction through sexy injections?
Mirrors an illusion, mirage forms of fusion.
Like Astral entities and storms.
Each of these shapeshifts forms.
All reality artificial illusions causing mental confusions.
Spiritually uplifting
Is sightings of unicorns.
Can payer or magic away corns
With prehistoric rhino horns?

WILD CURES

Every manmade cause has a cure. No matter malfunctions impure;
Hedgerow herbs, barks on trees, dock leaves nettle stings ease.
Each ailment an anecdote every digestion a lifeboat.
No accidents in the Universe…? See reality in reverse...?
Cancer cells karmically need to live.
On love's multiple levels learn to forgive.

SCRATCH MY BACK

Ann measured back against the wall.
Highly pleased each inch she more tall
Watching adults scratching their heads
Ones beaten in basketball,
Scratching wild bears without beating peers
Claim their most favoured trees,
Maybe one shared with honeybees.
Forage beetles, play, fornicate,
Eat sleep and ruminate,
Secure in forest estate?

VEILS

Creations' total circuits to complete.
All Souls' potential likely to deplete
Through minds' patterns to physicality
Swaying in seasons of duality
Till Love's equations achieved the more of God believed
The need for rising perceived.
Return to the Source when called
Negative nations more likely appalled
Negative Nature remerging…with…ALL…?

RABBIT RUN

Eating just wild rabbit without veg too long
Bodies depleted their health goes wrong.
Fibre and beta glucans health improves.
Oats sustainable as more horsepower proves.
Cutting greenhouse gases each year's resolution
Positively mixed with change
Made dark Moorish constitution. *Oaty milk* without sales talk
Ecologically walk their green walk.

AWARENESS AT WORK

All creatures make decisions
As to mating and provisions.

Is instinct better than thinking,
Intuition quicker at linking.

Though they might indulge in incest
Hen birds housekeep well their nest,
Sometimes hatching alien eggs
As jungle beasts drain pools to dregs.
Fear of survival made selfish
By killing one's rival?

COMPLETING V COMPETING?

How personalised quirks replicate, we're not able to duplicate,
Twin beasts will consume different feasts their own way
Folk saying, "Each dog will have its day."
Unique each choice…In its own voice
Due to early imitation, learning by invitation,
Every animal's Soul
Incomplete till all Creation again becomes WHOLE?

LAST WILL

Tough love too negative as solution?
Planetary like personal evolution
Needs changing climates
From volcanoes earthquakes tsunamis continental shits
Many problems manmade
Affecting lands from Peru to Adelaide.
Problems science explores, as our sea-chewed shores crumble,
All Creation benign blessed as humans grumble and grouse.
Love made man and louse.

RITUALS

Flint wood once was more precious than gold.
Reindeer antlers as picks.
Four-legged when upright crafted spears to fight
Building sacred sites, Pyramids Stonehenge and Rollright Stones,
Playing music with bears' bones
Worshipping sun and moon, solstice seasonal rites mid-June

As years fly on fast, too soon all is past

DE-NATURED

Cut jungles, those traumatising Nature's Mother
Kills one baby before yet another.
Sperm from males their offer neglected.
Panda mum in season mate rejected.
Human twins not parented divided, surrogate carers provided
Would their mum reject any three-inch cubs?
M/s panda nurtures babe though not hers as her broodiness stirs.

PINE

Arboreal athlete when starving.
Red squirrels for prey sharp teeth for carving,
Night hunters not dusk prowlers like Scotland's tabby-like wild cat.
Threatened their wilderness habitat, not for petting
Surviving without human vetting, solitary but always go-getting.
Few fears of death so less fretting.
For how long - worth betting?

GROUNDED

Winter winds tree's foliage relieves
Daydreamer Ann sees falling leaves
The higher tree's crown the deeper roots go down
For Mum's womb heaven she grieves.
As Grandad's tresses fall on dinner plates
Fearing his nearing death Ann daily hates.
Cooks healthy meals organic rice
With many a spice
Whatever the price.

SPINNERS - 1 -

Walks horses busses bikes
Eating less clean air hill hikes.

Electric cars on charge all night
Home insulation by right.
Coastal defences

Sun creams and parasols
Cosmic Souls stars and planets on same carousels

As volcanoes fertilise
Barren pastures past.

We aim to save skins
To outlast next nuclear blast.

SPINNERS - 2 -

Mammoth's mouth with undigested shoots of pine
Artic fossilised beasts to tropical food inclined
From Mercury Venus Mars Polar Lights spied
No light pollution puzzling birds
All galaxies aligned
Doughnut-shaped inhospitable till over-hot gasses cool
Hollow insides all spun on God's spool.
Of all Creation's heavens
Earth the lowest school?

GOOGLE-WORTHY

Coolest tree-hugging koalas fur-coated
Ferocious frog anger bloated.

Honeybirds lighter than paperclips
No wounds surgically stitched
Cheetah's purrs high-pitched
Heal fractured hips.

Penguin and puffin chicks
At speed fly underwater,
Flexible tail-udders allow agility
Competing with acrobatic seal cow's ability.

Male birth-giving angelfish show no misogyny.
Nature's amazing versatile progeny.

PEACE-MEAL?

Canadians now choosing peacekeeping to peace-making.
Military helicopters now for lifesaving from stormy seas.
Or mountain rescues manned so they're not
de-programmed
From their training as killing machines.
Peaceful climates improve all scenes.
Children playing war games
On hearing, 'You're dead!'
Laughing with fun
Spring up again with
Stick gun.

ELECTRO-MAGNETIC

Kilian photographs the invisible reveal
Electro-magnetic aura the sensitive feel
Dousing with copper rods
Seeking water below green sods. Plants emit unseen light
Beyond most human sight
Unless with psychic powers seeing fairy energy round
flowers.
How many planets can bear life physically?
How many faiths for Seekers questing quizzically?

REWARDING PAIN?

'Cutting…burning…hair-pulling…schoolkids make me sad,
Teachers, screechers, Grandad, all stressed, depressed...'

'Imitation follows empathy Ann, apes see no alternative than
Using grooming for soothing feelings.
Lonely zoo schools, biting bars, emit unnatural squealings.'
'Here I speak my mind, show my emotions
Girls' wounds covered-up.
Cuts me out to win…till I cuts meself in…'

PAIN REWARDING PAIN?

'Ann, we needn't repeat bad habits, make better choices
Than beasts In the field. They also feel stressed, unloved,
Rejected by mum like you, depressed. By predators oppressed
Their lives threatened at each moment.
Darling, put that knife away, please. ''I'm hearing voices…'
'Beware they don't take away your choices…'

PERMANENT PAIN?

'Self-harming won't appease your need to help those in
pain
Hoping blood flowing will help them growing into
Self-gain.
Ann, sing your own song.'
'Their choice. They sees nuffink wrong.'
'Life becomes Self-correcting by negativity rejecting.
Lonely needs to be strong and right.
So, all Self-inflicted pains are blight.'
'Right?'

VARIED VIEWPOINTS

'Viewpoints versatile some virtuous some vile.
Something right won't suit every lifestyle.
Truth in some cultures impolite - yet not to fight.
Wisdom's not valued like wealth
Not based on environment like one's health
Which parent good for everywhere
What children love if they won't share?'
Solomon lives. Ignorance love forgives.

LITTLE MIRACLES - 1 -

Mister Spider size of tiny rice grain
Suiter's romantic intention plain
Bright alluring dance shows love's peacock tail-fan
Post coital pregnant killer not his plan.
Leaf-cutting ants fresh underground
Fungus feeds crèche nest
As parents next generation breed
No carbon dioxide do they ingest
For waste factory fumes chimneys supplied

LITTLE MIRACLES - 2 -

Male mating surprise paper-clip size
On waterfalls' rock gushes drown calling croak
For an amorous bloke about to choke
He gracefully waves a long elegant leg
Hoping with princess he'll fertilize an egg.
Crop-circle pattern sand-shaped by pufferfish
Displayed for females motherhood their wish
Caring males give – Don't beg.

LITTLE MIRACLES - 3 -

World family's food-web won't survive our ocean plankton's demise
Half of earth's oxygen this flourishing they provide
Feeding krill - fish - whales…dolphins…
Sharks' catch as seabirds snatch
Hopefully soon before man's harpoon. Ruined plankton warns goodbye to all above.
'Thank God Grandad accepts rebirth as God's love.'

HAS BINS?

Seemingly uncontrolled chaos in flux
Some mouths silent while swimmer bird clucks
Some fish walk while dolphins fly
Most youngsters play avoiding rucks
Some mammals love wet some stay dry
Amazing multi-mixtures seen and unseen.
Let turtles live in safe shells
Whether buff mottled or green
Celebrate Creation's multitalented spells

HAS BINS?

Overcooked foods' disposal
Anaerobic or aerobic need selection
Central proposal separate collection
Saving landfill from meat and metals
Recycling batteries and kitchen kettles. Surplus cardboard in packs
Incompletely filled despite labelling gas capture wiser
Manufacturers still not billed since organic waste makes firtiliser
Long lice domestic compost
Homegrown wormery garden's oxidiser.

DREAMCOATS

See the sparkle in starlings and peacocks
Minerals glinting in fossilised rocks
Florescent hues flash ripples in seaweeds' playing fields.
Hear music in everything all organisms silently sing
As their journey they redefine.
Tinsel and sequins Paradise Birds outshine
Secret futures all creatures divine.

BIBLICAL?

No crater after an air-burst. Abraham witnessed it first
Fire and brimstone alarmingly green
Post atomic explosions trinitite was also seen.
Could Creator God curse all human sights as lowly
Knowing mankind might make blue skies holy?

Unknown energies where do they arise?
Mother Nature won't decide to commit suicide?

THIEVES?

Famished humanity grabs food no beastly behaviour seen as rude?
Surviving seagulls' sharp appetites rated as aggressive parasites,
Net-trawling stealing fish for fingers.
Starving rogue elephants' resentment lingers, towns
rampaged. Siberians' barometers overheating strange.
Reindeer trains 500 miles lichen-seeking exhausted by
climate change without mountain hiking. Late-born calves
tracking disliking

REVOLUTIONARY BIRTH

'Kill yourself? *Take* responsibility, Ann.
Every earth life part your Plan.'
'Life and death bad. Solve my problems, Grandad?
Never mind the World's. Never!'
'How dare you assume best answers not yours?
Even wild tigers lick their own sores
Nowhere to go but everywhere...
Find fun in the 'NOT fair'

REVELATION

'Live spirituality inside out, clear karma on blue globe's
roundabout. Endless are learning curves, despite wilful
swerves
Divinity no lover of doubt. Ann, ask your aunty Mable
She's a good Nature Studies Teacher
A family fable'
'You too Grandad. Telling me too limited every label.'

'Necessary Ann. End Times now unstable.

ELEVENTH HOUR?

'Grandad, what's true, climate change or...?'
'Global warming?'
'Warning. Too many emissions. Like money-grabbers.
I mean, what if it's all fake news?'

'Darling Ann cynicism based on no evidence is worse than
ignorance.' 'Like school, all based on fear of failing
And not fitting in. Why not wild life too?'

TWELTH HOUR?

12-year cycles between all cosmic crossroads
To save us mayflies glow-worms and natterjack toads
Soya not meat now causing forests denuded
Caused by caring vegan not excluded

As in UK cattle rustling, rustic drug-pushers hustling
Despite politicians' desperate bravado.
'Somewhere, Ann, in some time-zone
Life will continue to thrive
Alive – We're never alone!'

COOPERATIVES?

Coral reefs' produce half of all species
Psychedelic colonies teeming with acrylic deep-sea citizens
Mute or full-grown all linked and gifted inwardly synced
Exploring avoidable dangers with unwelcome strangers
Skittish incentive playful in teamwork no event baleful
Death no barrier to advancement
From polyps to pufferfish all permitting holy advancement.

BRAINY - 1 -

Humans wish for heaven not dead
Mental fears try not to die instead
Animals war without 'jaw' territorial like cavemen of yore
Seeing high skies some want to soar.
Planes quiet cool clean ionic wind Star Trek aircraft but
thin-finned
Oxygen disposed; edible meats' reposed
Beastly cruelty in slaughter rescind

BRAINY - 2 -

Tamed parrots will kiss their human carer
Interfering with Nature? Also, the seafarer?
The Milky Way's stars fewer than unique human brains
With only 200 billion neurons each.
Spider fearing plebs
Breaking their homely webs.
Beware over-harvesting every fish stock haul
Otters hold hands so love sustains all

PROTOTYPE?

Citizens struggle for breath. Plastics prefer a slow death.
1 in 8 eat without treated meat
Shorter-term sell-by-date than fracking.
Seaweed makes edible wrapping
Geothermal gas ready for recycling now.
Under 5 UK Councils if oil interests allow.
Saved pigs, holy cows graze, birds on more boughs
Serenading healthy days.

WHALE OF A TIME?

Poaching and habitat loss reversing
Numbers of Indian rhinos now not worsening.
Three third more wild tigers since 2007
Thanks to Sebangan Park Earthly Heaven.
For Indonesia's orang-utan tree climbing kin
World animal protection against ghost gear

Caught deep sea creatures soon won't disappear
Global traders allowing more to reappear

NATIONAL TRUST

Soon no longer will farmers lack
As 1940s strip field aids nationwide come back
Long stretch of coastline now a haven
For seabirds, guillemots, tern and raven.
Wildflowers as clover sorrel and cowslip
Badgers squirrels shrews dormice after long kip
National Trust with friends at Worms Head
Dolphins forging ahead,

A CIC

'You join ATMA Enterprises?'
'Grandad, their Playshops fit all sizes. Not full of misers.'
'Want *me* to pay Ann, for…MY MISSION ON EARTH?'
'Non-profit making Playshops. Not capitalists polluting
everywhere
'Heavy metal left behind. In poisoned water
They're now making healthy drinking!'
'Miracle thinking, adopted granddaughter, Ann!'
'Ta, adopted Granddad!'

BIO-DIVERSITY

Tourist attractions in Philippines' isles rain forest for miles
Sporting unique caterpillars, lizards, crocodiles, peacocks
Exporting versatile resin and citizens to our NHS to nurse
And homegrown beer while conservationists endear
Endangered species from the pet trade
As with cockatoos from Poachers and zoos.
No young farmers inheriting dad's spade

PROSPECTS

In money-mad people compassion can be slacking
Machines backing cash extracted from worldwide hacking
Oil and gas reserves, plus wildlife preserves
Strident supporters of rural fracking
Protesters not attacking.
Longevity in mountain air hidden hilltops shelter tigers so rare
God-eaters in highest Himalayas
Serving us preserving Earth with their prayers.

GRATITUDE

'Grandad you never boast I like that
Most often you walk or cycle leaving car
Never take a plane that's why you're not fat.'

'But maybe too vain to wear a bra.'

'Taught me lots like switch off at the mains.'

'Ann, seven geothermal areas in UK
Let's recycle in Crewe OK?'

HONEST WAYS

Mother Nature breeds deceivers but she won't lie
As historic regions of earth newly frazzled dry
Even though she's yet to learn her gifts don't die
Rendering extinct spiritually suspect.
With infinity let diehards expect
As the resurrection plants in desert puddles
Disentangle all man's mental muddles
And horror-filled huddles?

SEEING RED

Fewer snakes more poaching patrols
Mountain gorillas' population controls
Congo tourism on the red list. Save species not now missed.
Global bans in preparation
In every seafaring nation saved the fin whale from soup
For conservationists a celebrated scoop
Preventing the oceans' food-chain's links
As from paper straws civilisation drinks.

DARLING DANGERS

Ireland's Dusty Dolphin returns dropped cans
Land delivered, at hand adorning fans.

After shepherding injured swimmer
This almost human creature's no sinner.
When attacking a bathing lady intruder
Is blaming instinctive behaviour much cruder
Than Man's; Given female victim and Dusty forgave each
other
Dolphin greeting lady like her mother…?

EGG LAID BEACHES

Florescent sea-blue safires as aquatic bugs
Colour changing skills unlike our garden slugs
Effectively camouflaged they challenge science
Wee wafer-thin invertebrates in defiance
Defend themselves by seemingly disappearing.

Only human Assented Masters agree to l/earning
Spiritual physics until each prepared for turning
Invisible… disappears…
Like most of Creation's distant spheres

KILLING CLIMATES?

Porta Rica's politicians voted for green tourist attractions
Beach hatching sands not supporting hotel' high-heeled
While baby tortoises deceived by city lights' distractions
Leave moonlit sea for night traffic's killing field
Australia's night parrots for decades disappeared
And so ornithologists thought their demise sealed

Maybe the dodo has already reappeared?

MORNING GLORY

128+44 in 2018! Botanic scientists exploring life's range
To counter arboreal disease and vegetarian mange
Found hidden wild flora as in many new years gone by
To cure global patients' with multiple species as 44 fungi

Plus aquatic herbs brightening air aiding oxygen increase
Supporting trees. Optimism will never decrease.

LOVE NOT LANDFILL

One-day outfits ban. No man volcanoes can.
Byron's clothes still seen; poem DARKNESS read.
Sun and stars had fled. Again, world's swansong…?
Nostradamus got his death-date wrong!
Sunlight returned as did resurfacing island powers,
Old Masters painting recolonising flowers.
Greenery garnishing land,
Beaches sea-swept till…high tide returns golden sand.

VAN DE SANT

If Deborah a zebra her stripes would be green
The Meaden Empire recognises the Golden Mean.
She of Dragons' Den her fire scorching men.
Not he recycling plastic bottles and 20 bins
CED Innovations saving many fish-stock fins
From plastic ducks to corporations' desk chairs
In earth-friendly furniture commit shares?

PROFITS OF DOOM?

From Poland to both poles North and South
Coal fired fumes wafted by each world wind
Plentiful platitudes in each globe-warmed mouth
Pledges by profit seekers they'll rescind
Willow baskets with plastic bag policing.
Remedial measures are now increasing.
English grapes once filled Roman bellies
Artic picnics melting jellies?

HOLISTIC HARMONIES

Human stewards on Mother
Earth's frequencies integrate
These augmenting our green environments
Even unknown world villains resonate

Pines on mountains so speaking trees in wild woods
Ann supports hurt yobs hiding in hoods
Helps them be resilient like natural growth
Trusting youth more her heartfelt oath
Cherish all damaged childhoods

ENDLESS HORIZONS

'Serpents climb love's ladder much higher space-sent worms
With every sperm germ including rising therms
Infinity linked Ann in trance
Timely storks again in UK's romantic dance.
Dead wombs can give birth full worth
Invisible powers implementing the Plan. Your first baby Ann
Re-embodied Grandad back as a girl human.'

BEFORE BEYOND

'Establish your future's firm foundation.
Encourage ecological education. As tipping-point appears
Mankind reduces fears by way of hiding from truth too stark,
So encouraging global dark. Choking hearts and minds.
Ann where's more future hope you'll find when I leave you far behind in this domain?
Yet love will
Remain!'

SECOND SPRING?

Night-sweats and hot-flushes
Dead rivers
Word-loss dried rushes
Pastures parched
Early green leaves sun-starched
Depressed youths
Unproductive fields
Starvation
Devastation
Muffled bees
Mother Nature's menopause seeds Hope's yields
Sea rises desalinated world appetites please
For all Man and Japan
nuclear ban.

Not silent but sing
Second Spring
Humanity's New Plan!

REGENERATION

'From darkest fears Ann feel freed
Global Rays of Light seed uplifts all need
Chloroftourocarbons advised Greenpeace
Unprotected from dangerous ultraviolet light
Ozone hole currently heals
Hope in humanity's deals
Montreal Protocol optimism in sight
Signed by every national government on earth.'

'Grandad, let's now all believe in global rebirth!'

WORKS BY WRITER
CHRISTOPHER GILMORE

Actor, Author, Teacher, Learner

'Behind the Curtain' my real life-story won a 'Writer of the Year Award' from United Press 2010; who also published dozens of my poems. Other publishers featuring my works so far are ATMA Enterprises, Robin Books, Pegasus, Routledge Educational, Synectics Education Initiative and 6 books with CompletelyNovel.

Has over 30 plays and musicals performed, including 4 in fringe theatres in London as with Old Fruit, a two-hander at the King's Head -

'…Home counties Stringberg…' Michael Billington, The Guardian

and

'A deep, convincing play.' John Hewitt, Edinburgh Tel & Argus

A United Press Author of the Year 2010

Christopher Gilmore has long been at the forefront of the holistic and complementary education movements. He has long been using skills and experience gained as an actor, teacher and, as an author to help students of life and death and everything in between, utilise the multiple layers of meaning and experience they have available to them.

He is qualified in Brain Gym (EduK) and has run "Playshops" on Person-Centred skills on four continents, seeking happiness in all of life's lessons.

Christopher has written novels, self-help books, poetry, Talking Books as modern fables, plays and musicals, plus an opera called STONE THE HEART OF GOLD. His innovative approaches to life and learning have in all ways encouraged personal evolution through direct experience of one's own inter-dimensional energies. He is the Founder of ATMA Enterprises (C.I.C.) - A Social Enterprise Co-Creating innovative ways for people of all ages to expand their innate potential through person-centred experiential learning. The main offering in this programme named MY MASTER LEARNING MENU is a Self-evaluating quiz MINING ME.

07837 971 408
Christopher_Gilmore@ymail.com

34 Clifton Avenue
Crewe CW2 7PZ

www.CHRISTOPHERGILMORE.co.uk
www.ATMAENTERPRISES.org

SHOWS SEEKING PRODUCTION

LOVE ON THE POOLS

An old-style farce

LET'S HELP AN ACCIDENT

Student love affairs wants to adopt an Irish tramp

UNFROCKED

Celibate priest's affair with divorce, she aiming for priesthood

MUMS AND SONS ETC

Tarts at heart?
Two actors, three sexes, one pretty youth – up for adoption…?

MISTER MUM

Family musical on real-life bachelor fighting bureaucrats, he aiming to adopt ethnically diverse orphans

SEEKING COMPOSERS

JONATHAN

Oratorio of Jonathan Livingston Seagull, a ballet for athletes set in the gym

STONE THE HEART OF GOLD

2-act opera, Honeyville's debt-free citizens fight their dictator benefactor, Father Goldstone

PLAYS & MUSICALS STAGED

OLD FRUIT

Two-hander staged in Fringe London and Edinburgh Festival
"This witty and powerful account of marriage..." Yorkshire Post

FATAL FOREPLAY

Comedy on a rich self-made suicide

3 SCHOOL MUSICALS

OLD SCHOOL TIE	TELLING TALES	LILLYPUTLAND
WW2 refugees meet German convict - musical	Daydreamer Peter with fresh teacher disrupts classroom	Children fear the giant 2-act play with songs

SHANGRILA

2-act musical - Two Loves, Five Lives, One PASSION!
Choir presentations - professional CD available

FORWARD FANNY

Middle-age stroke-case marooned in a geriatric day-hospital

HOLY HAWK

Anti-nuclear student rag week, bishop kidnapped

ARGIE-BARDJI

Pakistani bit actor determined to play Hamlet in London's West End

CAESAR'S REVENGE

UK tour and Edinburgh and excerpts on BBC TV
A comedy on rebirth ghosted by that dead atheist, GBS!

SEARCH FOR SANTA

A large cast community Christmas show.

2 ISRAELI PLAYS IN ENGLISH

SOUND IN THE WILDERNESS Conflicts in new the kibbutz	WE'LL DIE TOMORROW Soldiers trapped in the middle of a mine field

THREE LUNCHTIME SHORT PLAYS PERFORMED IN LONDON'S FRINGE WEST END

SHALLOW END	TWO INTO ONE WON'T	TEST MATCH

KING OF SHADOWS

Moira Calldicott's poetic novel dramatised. 6th century Glastonbury quest. Power and submission, truth and deceit battle for supremacy.

Agent: James Church (+447919 821374)
jameschurch@hotmail.co.uk

CANADIAN CBC

3 TV PLAYS UNDER CONSIDERATION

GOODNIGHT ALL THE WINNERS	BUSKING BILL	EARLY AUTUMN OF A BLUE CANARY

Agent: Christine Shields (+447729619139)
shieldscimpacta@blueyonder.co.uk

YOUTUBES

5 REJUICED SHAKESPEARE

Written and performed by Christopher Gilmore

4 TALKS ON - Love Begins with Me

PUBLISHED BOOKS

TELLING TALES

Author reads audio book of fables for all the family - second edition

BRIGHT EYES AND BUBBLES

Author reads audio book of fables for all the family - second edition

ALICE IN WELFARELAND

A novel new-age nuclear faction

ALIVE ALIVE O

12 light-hearted animal stories featuring the Grinning Reaper!

WATCH THE BIRDIES

A feather fest of high flying avian fables

SOUL-CENTRED EDUCATION

Make your higher self more user-friendly. Third edition

FREE SCHOOLS - THAT'S THE SPIRIT???

Available on kindle

INDIGO EDUCATION - For All Ages!

Selling well interest in education being so wide

THE MUSHROOM MEN

20 Imperfect peace poems - CD in production

DOVETALES

10 Illustrated guidebooks for proactive lovers of Self-learning

ARTS WITHIN

Fewer Tears, Finer Sears?

GODLY GEOGRAPHY

Less Green Gloom, More Mother Love?

HOLISTIC HISTORY

Fewer Disasters, More Déjà vu?

INTEGRATED SCIENCE

Love Before Learning?

LOVING LANGUAGES

More Babel, Less Babble?

MIGHTY MATHEMATICS

More Fun, Less Fear?

MUSICAL MEDITATIONS

Octaves of Awareness?

RELIGIOUS EXPERIENCES

Dreams With The Supreme?

SPORTS, HEALTH & DANCE

More Grace, More Uplift?

TECHNOLOGY FOR ALL

Fewer Boxes, Further Bridges?

BOOKS SEEKING PUBLICATION

VOICELANDS

A Trilogy including CAMPUS VOICES, NORDIC VOICES and ASIAN VOICES.
From rape to revelations, controversial explorations of mental distress.

SHANGRILA REVIVED - Novel (Offer under consideration)
Real-life story of a unique O.A.P. with toy-boy writing an original musical. Was considered by UK's National Theatre, professional CD available on request.

ANN OF GREEN FABLES

Including PAN SPEAKS ON EARTH
Interactive ballads in 375 ecological mini-sagas in rhyme

9 NAUGHTY NEW-AGE NURSERY RHYMES

Seeking cartoon illustrator
Ballads to make you giggle!

LEARNING WITH LIMERICKS AND OTHER POEMS

"Insightful Inspiring and Instructive"
2 new Limericks published daily on social media

THE EYES HAVE IT - Novel
Dangerous expose of atrocities during the Troubles in Northern Island

UNDEREDUCATED - IN COSMIC CLASSROOMS

Behind the Chalkface

Lightning Source UK Ltd.
Milton Keynes UK
UKHW050332201119
353839UK00002B/2/P

9 781786 236043